SWEET SMELL OF REVENGE

PAM CLIFFORD

Sweet Smell of Revenge

Copyright © 2019 Pam Clifford

The right of Pam Clifford to be identified as the Author of the Work has been asserted by her in accordance with the Copyright, Designs and Patents Act 1988.

All the characters in this book are fictitious and any resemblance to actual persons, living or dead, is purely coincidental.

All rights reserved. Any unauthorised broadcasting, public performance, copying or recording will constitute an infringement of copyright. No part of this book may be reproduced or transmitted in any form or by any means, electronically or mechanical, including photocopying, fax, data transmittal, internet site, recording or any information storage or retrieval system without the express permission of the author.

All rights reserved.

ISBN: 978-1-6862-6321-7

To Tim, Dawn & Tracey

My thanks go to:

My editor, Lorraine Swoboda, whose professional eye for detail, encouragement and help has been invaluable and without whom my dream would never have become a reality.

Dawn Johnson for designing my cover.

My family for believing in me

Mark Salf for helping me understand the tachograph/digicard and how it affects drivers hours.

Stefan Van Jaarsveld for his suggestions and for explaining the properties of hazardous chemicals.

My Chums in alphabetical order: Debs, Deborah, Dell, Denise, Donna, Janet, Jenny, Lorraine, Maeve, Nette, Sandra & Shirley for your support and encouragement.

MONDAY 29TH APRIL

Morning

Tony left the house, quietly closing the door behind him. He didn't want to disturb Susan when she must have had a bad night too. They should never have gone to bed on an argument; he knew that. It was the one useful piece of advice his father had given him on his wedding day.

He headed for the Toyota and put his overnight bag into the boot, pausing to cast a quick glance up at the bedroom window. He had a long journey ahead of him and it would be tomorrow evening before he would be home again. Well, there was nothing he could do about that now.

It was only a short journey to the depot of the haulage company where he worked. His unit was loaded and ready for him, so he just had to call in at the office to get his notes.

"Hi, Craig, have you got my paperwork?"

The young traffic clerk, who was busy surfing the internet, got up reluctantly and picked up the run sheet.

"There's a slight alteration," he said. "An extra pickup to make from a new customer in Longburrow; came in early this morning. Just one pallet of hazardous to go to Leeds. He'll pay cash as he's not opened an account yet – the details are in your folder. We've left room at the back for it."

"That'll make me late for the pickup in Carlisle."

"It's not that big a diversion. Just let us know how you're getting on. We can ring them and let them know."

Tony sighed, and strode off down the yard to check his load.

Once in his cab, he flipped through his notes and studied the details of the first pickup. He wasn't happy with this extra job; it was in a village ten miles off, and a good fifteen minutes out of his way, which would set him back for the rest of the day. He returned the papers to the folder and set it on the passenger seat, then fired up the engine.

Once on the familiar main road out of town, he reached to turn on the radio for the sports news and settled in for a long day at the wheel.

"Oh, no!" he muttered. Cars were queuing and brake lights were coming on ahead. "This day's just getting better and better. I hope it's not an accident."

A herd of cows had escaped from a field and were creating a mobile roadblock. Bugger! He ran his fingers through his mop of dark curls in frustration. The police were already on the scene, trying to get on top of the situation, but the cattle weren't keen to follow orders. It was some few minutes before the traffic was beckoned on and Tony was once again sailing along the open road.

Cotswold Chemicals wasn't easy to find. The paperwork said it was a unit on somewhere called Bullnose Farm. Seeing a man walking his dog, Tony slowed down to ask for directions.

"Ah, yes," the man said, "it's that new development. Take the first turn right and look for a post box. Almost opposite on the left-hand side there's a track. You need to go up there for about half a mile."

He found the farm as instructed, but couldn't see any unit bearing the name of Cotswold Chemicals. He tried the door of the first one, belonging to Juicy Fruits Drinks, and found a pretty young girl tapping away at a computer.

She looked up as he walked in. "Can I help?"

"Is there a firm called Cotswold Chemicals hereabouts?"

"Someone moved into the end barn over there, I think," she said, pointing. "That might be it."

Tony thanked her and followed her directions.

As he approached, a scruffy young man came out of the unit and strode towards him.

"Cotswold Chemicals?" Tony called.

"Yes." He looked beyond Tony to his vehicle. "You'll need to reverse up to the unit as I don't have a forklift yet."

Tony lowered the tail lift as the man wheeled out a pallet of plastic drums on a hand-truck. This would make it difficult at the next drop as it would be in the way of the tail lift delivery. It was a good job there was still room left at the back to put this pallet.

Tony took over and maneuvered the load onto the platform to raise it to the lorry bed.

The man waited impatiently until the pallet was safely on board, and thrust an envelope into Tony's hand.

"Here's the money."

Tony did a quick count of the notes and stuffed the envelope into his pocket. "Where's the paperwork, mate?"

"Sorry, yeah, I forgot. I'll go and get it for you."

Tony busied himself putting up the orange hazardous load plates on his vehicle ready to set off, then started towards the door just as the man came out clutching a piece of paper with the details of the goods on his pallet. He had written the name and address at the top and it had all the relevant hazardous details required, but, as Tony pointed out, it wasn't proper headed paper. "I've only just started up the business," he said, "and my stationery order hasn't arrived yet."

Tony grabbed the paper and jumped up into the cab. After filing it in the documents wallet he reached for his phone.

"Can I speak to Craig, Jenny?"

"Yes, sure. I'll put you through."

"Hello, Craig speaking."

"Hi, it's Tony here. I've finally picked up that job at Longburrow."

"What kept you?"

"There was a herd of cows on the road, then it took a time to find the farm, and then I had to wait for their scrappy excuse for paperwork."

"Give us a ring when you stop for lunch."

"Okay, speak to you later." With no further interruptions, he should make it to the first motorway services in time for his first statutory tacho break.

He hadn't been underway long when the cab phone started to ring, so he switched off the radio and answered the call on hands-free.

"Hey, Tony, it's Leo."

"Hi, mate. Where are you today? Didn't see you in the yard this morning."

"No, I had a later start. Pongo rang in sick and I'm now taking his load up to Glasgow."

"I'm on my way to Carlisle via Sheffield, Leeds and Skipton, and I'm running later than I would have liked. The Leeds drop is an extra they lumbered me with this morning."

"Tell me about it! Are you home on Friday?"

"Yeah. See you in the Lion at seven o'clock?"

"Right-oh."

Tony hung up and turned the radio back on. A bit of music would help the miles pass.

Traffic was heavy around Coventry, but otherwise it wasn't a bad run. At the first motorway services on the M1, he pulled into the lorry park and made his way inside. He bought a copy of the Sun, picked up a cheeseburger and a coke, and sat on a bench to enjoy them. His vehicle was his pride and joy, and his home when he was on an overnighter, and he liked to keep it spotless. He hurled the empties into the bin, climbed back on board, and spent the last few minutes of his break reading the back pages before he fired up the engine and headed towards the industrial north.

He'd been trying to forget the argument he'd had with Susan last night, all over something and nothing. Her mother wanted to take them on holiday to Benidorm, and although he would like a break and the old gal was paying, his idea of a holiday and his mother-in-law's were totally different, and he'd point blank refused to go. He was now well and truly in the doghouse and would have to do some grovelling before he would be forgiven for his outburst.

Had he been too quick to dismiss the holiday offer last night? He should have taken time to talk it through with Susan. He'd never really wanted to go abroad. It wasn't that he was scared of flying or anything like that but he preferred the English climate which was far kinder to his fair skin. What did they eat over there? Nothing he would like, that was for certain. He'd heard tales of people getting stomach upsets from all that foreign food. Give him a roast dinner any day, or fish and chips on the prom. Also, he couldn't speak the language, so what was the point? He shouldn't stop Susan and the kids from going, though; it could be educational as well as fun for the children. He'd have to give it some more thought.

After about an hour, as he was nearing Sutton in Ashfield, there was a news flash on the radio. An artic had shed its load across two lanes of the M1 northbound, south of Sheffield, causing disruption and very slow traffic. Tony decided to come off at Chesterfield and take the A61 instead.

Through no fault of his own, he was really late for his first drop; and they had a new fork-lift driver who had only just got his licence and couldn't be hurried, so it was a while before he was back on the motorway again and heading for Leeds.

He would find somewhere to park up to take his lunch break once he'd dropped off the Leeds pallet, and he'd ring Susan and clear the air. Maybe she and the kids could go to Spain with her mother and then they could enjoy their usual Cornish holiday together later in the summer. He could fend for himself for a week. Yes, that was a plan; he would suggest that to her when they spoke.

With his exit road coming up, Tony signalled to leave the motorway, and was nearly taken out by a Beamer which cut him up, forcing him to brake hard. "Bloody idiot!" he yelled.

His drop was just outside the city on an old run-down farm. Tony located the premises, an almost derelict-looking barn with the doors shut and a dark blue car outside. He decided to ring the office before going off to look for someone.

"Craig, it's Tony."

"Hi, Tony. How you getting on?"

"I've just got to my second drop. It's a bit of a dive. I'm going to have my lunch break here so should be at the last one in Skipton around four o'clock."

"Fine."

"I'll be too late to do the pickup in Carlisle today, so I'll make an early start tomorrow and I'll be on their doorstep at start of play for their collection."

"Okay. See you tomorrow evening then."

Tony left his cab and tried the barn door, but it was locked. A voice from inside hollered, "Reverse up and I'll get the doors opened."

Tony started the engine and did as he was bid, then grabbed the paperwork in his folder and clambered out of the cab. As he turned and hopped onto the tail lift ready to unload the pallet, he noticed that the building was pretty much empty. Still, that wasn't his problem, so long as the papers were in order.

Craig's day had not begun well. His temperamental car had refused to start this morning and he was lucky to have been able to borrow his mother's for the short drive into work.

The phones were already ringing when he'd got there, and since then there had been one problem after another. He had been forced to add a drop to Tony's load that he hadn't been best pleased about, but he had left the yard now and was on his way.

Finally, things had quietened down, and while he waited for the rest of the drivers to come and collect their folders, he went back to his computer and started to surf the holiday companies looking for a bargain break for the end of July. He needed some sunshine, and his girlfriend, Carrie, had hinted that she would like to get away for a week during the factory fortnight, when traditionally factories closed completely for two weeks. Sun, sea and sex – yeah, that appealed to him.

The phone began ringing again, and he grabbed it impatiently.

"Grahams Transport, Craig speaking."

It was Andy ringing in sick, and unable to do the Scottish run as scheduled. Probably had a skinful yesterday, he thought, as he looked up Leo's home number. A Class One licence holder, which meant he was able to drive any of their vehicles including the articulated lorries, he was scheduled on later for local deliveries, but he agreed to come straight in. He preferred the long runs, and was always happy to have a night out. With a TV and his bedding in his cab it was like a home from home, and he always had an overnight bag packed, just in case.

One by one the drivers came in and collected their work sheets. There was plenty of Monday morning banter, mostly on the subject of the weekend's football matches. Craig dealt with several phone calls during this time, adding an extra collection, and emailing a proof of delivery to a customer for a job they had done last week.

With the last man out of the yard and on his way, Craig had just found the ideal holiday in Ibiza when the phone rang. It was Tony, complaining about the last-minute job he'd been given. No forklift – Craig should have asked about that, he said. He was running a bit late now, but was pushing on towards the motorway so no real harm done.

Trevor, the manager, arrived and started sorting the routes out for the following day. Craig filled him in on the various changes, then gathered together the drivers' timesheets from the desk and took them through to Jenny, the part-timer who was responsible for the accounts and wages.

"Thanks, love," she called from the little kitchen next to her office. "Did you have a nice weekend?"

"I played football for the Firsts on Saturday, and we won 2-1. I set up the first goal. Cassie and I went to that new club in town in the evening to celebrate. How about you?"

"Had my grandson to stay," she smiled. "We had a great time. He's growing up so fast though; it doesn't seem five minutes since he was born."

Trevor walked in, thumbing through a file. "I wonder if Andy will be back tomorrow, because I've got a nice full load from High Wycombe to Halifax which will suit him perfectly."

"Said he'd got a stomach upset. It might just be a twenty-four-hour bug, or more likely a drop too much last night," Craig surmised, "so he probably will be."

Jenny brought them both coffees, and retreated into her office.

Craig watched jealously as Trevor enjoyed a sausage roll with his drink. He would have to wait for the mobile sandwich seller to arrive later.

After the busy start, it was a fairly quiet morning with a few phone calls, faxes and e-mails with new jobs to be entered up and routed for tomorrow.

Jenny brought them both another cup of coffee as she left for home. She only worked mornings and told them she was off to make a cake for her WI meeting that evening.

"Bring us some in, Jen," Trevor called after her.

"I might if I have time," was the reply as she threw her handbag onto her shoulder and made for the door.

Monday morning and Frank Jarvis was happy to be heading in to work. Things were really looking up for the company. Today he had a meeting with a firm he had been trying to get into for the past year, and if he cracked this deal his profit margins could only soar.

It had been tough starting his chemical firm in Milton Keynes after being forced to move south to be nearer to his wife's ailing parents, but it looked as though the long hours and hard graft had finally paid off.

He was always first at the unit and usually the last to leave. He unlocked the office door and headed for the coffee filter machine and very soon had the delicious aroma filling the room. He booted up his computer and found the notes he had made for today's meeting with the restaurant chain who he hoped would help him make his name, as they were growing fast, opening a new venue every month. His cleaning fluids could be going to every corner of the country.

As he helped himself to his first coffee of the day, Frank heard a vehicle pull up outside. His wife and business partner, Jane, ambled in. While he concentrated on sales and the logistical side of the business, Jane, a trained bookkeeper, took care of the accounts. This morning she had the joys of the VAT return to look forward to. He was glad he had an excuse to get out of her way as she was never in the best of moods when that had to be done.

"Oh, good, you've got the coffee on."

Frank poured a mug and handed it to her, then settled back down to print off his notes for the meeting. Nothing happened. He punched the print button again: still nothing.

"Bloody printer!"

"Try re-booting the computer," Jane suggested, and he did so, with the same non-result.

"Where's Techie this morning?" he asked

"He isn't in until tomorrow. He's having a long weekend."

Techie, real name Jason, was setting up a website for the firm and had proved very useful, in the short time he had been with them, whenever errors appeared on the computer screen.

"I'll have to take my scribbled notes with me then," Frank grumbled. "I'll get him to look at the printer tomorrow."

There was no time for another coffee. He searched his drawers for the notes, grabbed some brochures, and kissed his wife goodbye before heading out to his Volvo to set off for his 10 o'clock meeting.

The phones were quiet, and Jane was able to make good progress with logging the last few invoices onto her computer ready to complete the VAT form. She hoped this morning's meeting went well as it would really boost their business.

It had been hard for Frank to give up his secure job in the north east, but since her dad had suffered a stroke, her mother needed her help. Although mentally he was fully recovered, he had been left in a wheelchair, and Jane had felt it was necessary to move down to be near them. Frank had been really supportive, which made it all that much easier. Their son, Michael, had soon settled into his new school, had taken his A levels and had recently started an apprenticeship with a local engineering company. She believed that the move had been good for all of them.

Her mind was wandering, and the columns didn't like it. Running her fingers through her short auburn hair, she stomped off to get another coffee to help her concentrate. She checked each row with the help of her calculator and soon found the invoice she had entered wrongly. With that corrected and everything beautifully balanced she entered all the figures onto the return. She loved it when numbers added up just as they should.

A jubilant Frank arrived back just before lunch to announce that the meeting had gone very well and that they were going to get the contract. It had been necessary to do a deal on the prices but he had secured their first order for June. All he had to do now was to find a haulage firm who could take the goods for him. Until now, he had only sold locally and was able to deliver those orders with a couple of part-time drivers in a van and a pickup truck.

As he was reaching for the yellow pages the door opened and Ian Herbert came in. In his early sixties, he looked a lot older, probably due to his thirty-a-day cigarette habit. Ian had come to work for Frank when he had first set up shop two years ago. He had a Hazardous Chemical licence, which was needed to transport by road any goods which were deemed dangerous, of which they shipped a small number.

"Hello, Ian. Have a good weekend?" Frank said, looking up.

"Yes, thanks. Got my spuds planted. You?"

"Had a good round of golf yesterday with Jane. Just a friendly with another couple, but it went well."

"Where am I off to today?" Ian asked.

"There's a pallet of peroxide ready-loaded on the truck to be delivered to Bedford. I'll just get the paperwork."

Frank told Ian about the new contract he had won that morning and asked him whether he wanted any more hours. He was a good, reliable chap and Frank liked him, but Ian wasn't keen on the idea of extra hours; his allotment needed a lot of work to keep it in good shape. He said he would think about it. Frank asked him to let him know as soon as possible as he would need to offer them to Tim, his other part-timer.

"Well, I'd better get off," he said, and lifting the keys from the board on the wall, he sauntered off round to the yard where the little pickup truck was kept. The gates were wide open, which they shouldn't be at this time of day.

His first thought was that Mike must have forgotten to relock the yard when he took the truck back after loading it. That lad would lose his head if it wasn't screwed on.

Then he realised that the vehicle was nowhere to be seen.

"Oh gawd! It must've been nicked!" He rushed back round to the office.

"The truck isn't there," he panted as he pushed in through the door.

"What do you mean, it's not there?" demanded a startled Frank.

"What I said. It's not there."

Frank charged out towards the yard, and found it empty.

Racing back to the office he asked his wife what number he should ring for the police. She said she thought it would be the local police station as 999 was for emergencies only.

"This is a bloody emergency!" he cried, but she found the local number and handed it to him.

"Calm down, and call Mike first," she said.

Frank took a deep breath, and phoned his son. He had been helping his dad to pick and pack the orders on Friday afternoon because the warehouseman was away sunning himself in Greece. Mike only worked at his usual job until noon on a Friday, and he needed some extra spending money for the weekend.

"Did you forget to lock the yard on Friday?" Frank barked as soon as Mike answered.

"No, of course I didn't. It was the last thing I did."

"Well, the bloody pickup's been nicked!"

"No! I definitely locked the yard on Friday and took the key straight back to the office."

"I'm worried about that lad," Frank said, as he put down the receiver. "I don't like that crowd he's started hanging round with. I know he was in a hurry to catch his train on Friday night and it wouldn't surprise me if he did forget to lock the yard."

He dialled the number Jane had given him and was put through to a Sergeant Willis, who asked a lot of questions, and then told him that he would send a constable out later that day.

"Whatever *later* is supposed to mean," he grumbled as he hung up. "Can you look up Chapman's Van Hire for me? I need to get another pallet made up and sent to Bedford. I promised it to them this afternoon and I don't want to let them down."

Jane Googled the number and arranged to hire a van for the rest of the day; then she drove Ian round to collect it while Frank went into the warehouse to set about loading up a new pallet.

The shrill ring of his alarm clock woke Richard with a start. Monday morning already, and another week in that stuffy warehouse to look forward to. He was glad to have got a job when he moved here from Leeds last year, but it was a bit monotonous, and that old fogey of a manager was a right grumpy old bugger. His head was aching. He'd had one too many down the Dog and Bone last night, though it was the same story pretty much every Monday morning. It would be good to ring in sick, but then he would only have to face the music tomorrow; so he might as well put on a brave face. He threw back the duvet, clutched his head, and headed for the shower.

Feeling a bit better, he wandered into the garden for his first fag of the day. There would be just time after breakfast to nip into the shop by the bus stop for a paper.

The bus dropped him a short walk from the industrial estate. The sun was shining and Richard was feeling a lot more human. All too soon he was standing outside the warehouse roller shutter doors, ready to start another week slaving for Bennett's Clothing.

"You have caused me no end of trouble this morning," hollered Old Henry as soon as he saw him. "You sent that shipment of jeans to the invoice address instead of their warehouse. It's going to be tomorrow before they get it now, and we've got to pay for it to be re-routed. I ought to take it out of your wages."

Richard muttered his apologies and decided to keep a low profile for the rest of the morning. He collected the orders from the tray on his desk and headed off to start picking and packing them.

He had a dreadful thirst, and after completing a couple of orders headed for the drinks machine and got himself a latte, and a sweet white tea for Henry. It wouldn't hurt to try and butter him up after the rocky start.

"Cheers, mate," Henry grunted. "There's a consignment of tee shirts due in at eleven. How are the orders going?"

"I've got a couple done, so there's just the big order to do for James Young and that back order for Glovers."

"I've got a meeting to go to at half ten, so make sure you check off that load from Turkey. They were five boxes short last time. Bloody driver on the make, I reckon."

James Young was a good customer with half a dozen shops in the South East. Checking them off as he went, Richard soon had the boxes palletised and wrapped ready to be picked up in the afternoon.

The Turkish vehicle was late and Henry was back before it arrived, which suited him very well. He liked to check the orders in himself as he found it hard to trust anyone else to do it. He had been working for the company for years and was well respected by the boss for his attention to detail.

A few more orders came down from the sales office, and the morning progressed, with Richard picking and Henry logging the new stock onto the computer system.

The nearby church bell struck one o'clock, so Richard grabbed his paper and lunch and made his way out to the landscaped seating area on the edge of the industrial estate, made reasonably pleasant with a few bushes and some benches. Henry went and sat in his car.

As Richard munched his sandwiches, he reflected on how lucky he really was. He enjoyed his job, even though Henry could be a miserable old fart at times. It was certainly a lot less stressful than it had been running his own business.

He picked up his wrappers, tossed them into the bin, and returned to the bench to read his paper and smoke a well-deserved cigarette.

MONDAY 29TH APRIL

Afternoon

It had been a busy morning for Susan Hedges at the veterinary practice, and she hadn't had time to dwell on the row she'd had with Tony last night.

Last to leave, as Mr Gregory had been called out to a cow with mastitis, and surgery had finished an hour ago, she locked up and made her way to her little red Micra. She loved her work as receptionist, but she really wanted to be a veterinary nurse when the kids were older.

As she started the engine her mind went back to the angry exchange last night and she bitterly regretted flouncing off to bed as she had. She had been so excited when her mother offered to pay for them all to go to Spain with her and she'd assumed Tony would be too. She couldn't understand why he was being so stupid and selfish. He wanted to rent a caravan in Cornwall, as they had in previous years. Why couldn't he see that this was a great adventure they had been offered? They could go to Cornwall any other time. She still felt bad about her reaction, though, and would try to talk it over with him when he rang at lunchtime, as he always did, to let her know how his day was going and to ask about hers.

Back home by 12.45, Susan picked up the post, and finding an envelope from her sister, which could only be a birthday card for Gina, quickly hid it in the hall cabinet. She put the kettle on and made a sandwich to enjoy while she watched the news. Tony would ring soon and she could apologise for her outburst.

Selecting an apple from the fruit bowl, she picked up her iPad to check on a top she was watching on eBay. Still no bids on it – she would put in one tomorrow morning before work. Glancing at the clock, she wondered why Tony hadn't rung yet. Sometimes he was later than others; it depended on where they had sent him. She knew he was going to end up in Cumbria tonight so he was probably taking a later break.

She put on a Keane CD and fried off the mince and onions for a lasagne. They always had pasta of some sort on a Monday because it was something Tony didn't like. He was a traditional English meat and two veg man: 'none of that foreign muck,' as he put it. When Keane started singing about the Sovereign Light Cafe her thoughts went back to holidays and the happy times they'd had. She could understand that Tony would be reluctant to go on holiday with her mother. He loved the British seaside, and watching *Benidorm* on TV hadn't endeared the place to him; but the beaches and sun would be so nice, especially after the cold winter they had been through.

The phone rang and she dashed to answer it. It wasn't Tony. Her mother wanted to know if she had asked him about her proposed holiday invitation. Susan, at a loss as to how to answer the question without getting into things she would rather not discuss, decided to tell her that she hadn't had chance and would do so tomorrow when he came home from his trip. After chatting for a while Susan replaced the phone onto its base, wondering if Tony had tried to ring while she was talking.

Deciding to tackle the big basket of ironing, she set up the board, changed the CD to a more upbeat Queen album, and set about her least favourite task.

Gina was the first to arrive home from school and burst through the door asking if there was any post for her and what was for tea. Susan told her it was lasagne, carefully avoiding the question of post. Grabbing a packet of crisps from the bag on the kitchen worktop Gina raced off to her room to get changed out of her uniform.

Susan layered the pasta sheets and mince mixture, topped it off with a jar of white sauce, and slid the dish into the oven.

A little later John came bounding in and dumped his football kit in the middle of the kitchen floor.

"We beat them!" he cried. "And I got one of the goals!"

"Well done! Now put your dirty kit into the wash basket and hang your bag up," replied his mother. "Dinner will be ready at half past five."

With a shrug John did as he was told and made his way upstairs to change.

Susan returned to the last of the ironing and soon had it finished. She would reward herself with a glass of red later.

It was five o'clock, and still there was no call from Tony. She was beginning to feel annoyed and worried at the same time. She picked up the phone and dialled his number, but was sent straight to voicemail. He didn't usually turn his phone off as he had hands-free kit and the office might need to contact him. She left a message for him to ring her.

With garlic bread in the oven, she set about preparing the salad.

A delicious aroma filled the air as she called the kids down for their dinner.

John was first at the table, claiming he was starving, and soon they were enjoying their meal and chattering about their day.

"We're starting the end of term play next week," Gina said. "I'm hoping to get a part at the auditions tomorrow."

"What play are they doing this year?" Susan asked.

"I don't know yet; Mrs Butcher has written it."

When they had finished their meal, Susan stacked the plates into the dishwasher and the kids went off to do their homework, while she listened for the phone.

Ian returned with the hire van, and he was soon loaded and on his way.

Frank was logging all the details for his new account onto his computer. They would e-mail through their first order on Monday, 3rd June, so that would give him good time to find a firm who would be able to take his goods to far flung parts of the UK. They had promised to send him the addresses of their restaurants so that he could get some quotes from local hauliers, and see which ones he could do with his own vehicle.

Jane soon arrived carrying a bag from the local deli. She handed it to Frank and went to the small kitchen to get them both a drink.

"What do you think has happened to the pickup?" Jane asked, setting his mug in front of him.

"I don't know." Frank picked the slices of cucumber out of his baguette. "That stupid boy must have left the keys in the ignition too."

Privately, Jane was worried about some of the friends that their son had started to hang around with. She had heard at the hairdresser's last week that one of them had been in trouble with the police recently over drugs, and she really hoped that Michael hadn't started down that slippery slope. It seemed disloyal to say so, though; she preferred to give her son the benefit of the doubt, at this stage at least.

Frank picked up the phone and dialled the first number on his list: a local haulier, who told him that they handled small orders locally and only took full loads further afield. Next was a pallet carrier with depots throughout the country, but they couldn't handle some of his cleaning products. He knew they were hazardous by road and was fully conversant with the laws on the paperwork for such goods, but hadn't realised that a lot of nationwide outfits didn't carry dangerous goods. The person he spoke to explained that it was mainly due to the cost of getting their drivers trained and licensed. "And it's not a good idea to have, say, a thousand litre container of formaldehyde travelling next to a pallet of coconut cookies," the man said with a laugh.

So it was back to the drawing board. He found a firm called HAZ-R-US who seemed to fit the bill. They would get a Mr Jenkins, their sales executive from the local depot, to phone him back.

Late in the afternoon, Jane set off for home to prepare their evening meal, leaving Frank still waiting for the police to arrive. He would need to get a case number before he could start trying to make a claim on the insurance, although it didn't seem likely that he would be able to get a cent out of them if his lad had left the truck open and available for any Tom, Dick or Harry to come along and take it.

Mr Jenkins phoned him and took the details of the goods he was intending to ship. As Frank didn't have the destinations yet, the haulier told him that he would come back with prices for different zones around the country. He would be round that way on Friday and would drop by to see him.

A few minutes later, there was a knock at the door, and Frank looked out to see a police car parked outside. He let the constable in and showed him to a chair.

"Can I make you a cup of tea?"

"No, thanks, sir. Once I'm done here, I'm off home for an early night for once."

Frank took his seat behind the desk as the policeman took out his notebook.

"So, I understand a van has gone missing?"

Frank nodded, and gave him the vehicle's details and registration number. "It was loaded up on Friday evening ready for today's run, with a pallet of peroxide for a group of hair salons."

"Who loaded the vehicle?"

"My son; and he insists that he locked up the compound and brought the keys back in here. Well, they were certainly here when my driver, Ian Herbert, came in. Unfortunately he found the compound was unlocked when he went round to take the load to Bedford at lunch time."

"We will need to speak to your son. What time does he finish work?"

"4.30."

"I'll come and see him here tomorrow evening at six o'clock. Could you give me Ian Herbert's address?"

Frank told him and he wrote it down.

"A description of the vehicle will be logged onto the computer system, and I'll keep you up to date with any developments," the policeman said as he got up to leave.

Frank walked round the office turning everything off, and made his way to the door, not feeling very optimistic of ever seeing his pickup again.

Richard had got on pretty well this morning and had most of the pallets ready to be collected this afternoon.

"There's a couple of new orders for you in the tray," Henry informed him when he came back from his lunch break.

He picked up the paperwork and flicked through it. There was a small local order, and he would pick that one up himself. The other was a larger one for an outdoor pursuits franchise in the Yorkshire Dales. He started collecting the goods together for the two deliveries while Henry worked in his little office.

The door opened and Richard looked up to see Claire from Sales. She was in her mid- twenties, he guessed, with long, dark hair and an hour-glass figure; he was pretty sure she had the hots for him. He hadn't been interested in looking for love since losing his wife. He had only just started to get his life back together. Maybe he would ask her out one day, but not yet.

Claire smiled sweetly at him and asked if he had time to put together a small order. It was for a new client and she really would like to get it sent out today to impress him.

He held out his hand for the paperwork. "I should be able to manage that."

He stuck his head round the office door to inform his boss. "I think I've got time to get it sorted if you can put it on DHL's system."

Grudgingly Henry took the piece of paper which Richard held out.

"I've got enough to do with getting this stock ready to put away. It's about time you learnt how to do it. Remind me to show you tomorrow when I've got a spare half-hour."

By the time the clock on the warehouse wall showed five o'clock, Richard had achieved everything he needed to do. He strode out towards the main road with his jacket over his shoulder.

The bus was late and there was only standing room as usual. He found himself a place near the front and watched the fields speed by. It seemed that everyone around him was in a bad mood: the exasperated mother trying to keep her bored toddler amused, the vacant-looking chap standing next to him who reached up to hold onto the strap to keep his balance and smelt of more than one days' lack of washing, and teenagers arguing loudly at the back of the bus.

By the time he arrived at his village stop he was feeling hot, fed up and in need of some fresh air. He lit a cigarette and set off down the narrow lane, and was enjoying the peace and quiet when he noticed a dark green lorry parked right outside his house.

"Sodding cheek!" With no footpath, and his front door opening straight out onto the road, it was blocking the light and the warmth of the late afternoon sun from his living room window, and he would be forced to put the heating on.

As he drew closer, he saw that the bonnet was up. It must have broken down, but there was no sign of a driver. He would fetch a pen and paper and take down the company's name and phone number and find out when it was going to be moved.

Richard fished in his pockets for his house keys and stepped into his home. There was an awful sickly-sweet smell as he closed the front door, as if a cat had been shut in and peed somewhere. "That's all I need!" he said, and headed for the kitchen.

MONDAY 29TH APRIL

Evening

As Craig had started early today, he'd headed off at four in the direction of the travel agents to pick up a few brochures, leaving Trevor to man the fort and de-brief the remaining drivers as they came back. It was generally a quiet time between then and six, and the paperwork was complete for tomorrow's runs, so Trevor was just making himself a coffee when the phone summoned him back to his desk.

"Grahams Transport," he barked.

It was Severn Bore Brewery, who wanted to know why their four pallets of ale had not been delivered to Skipton yet. The beer festival was tomorrow and they were waiting for them.

"They should be there by now," Trevor said. "Tony hasn't rung through with any problems since his last drop. Let me just give him a call and see what's what."

Using the other line he dialled Tony's number. It rang and rang before switching to voice mail. He left a message.

He returned to the caller. "Sorry about this. I can't get through to him just at the moment. He's got the right address, so I can't see that there's a problem. I'll call you as soon as he gets back to me." He replaced the receiver, and checked his computer for any traffic snags which could have caused the delay, but there were no reports of any major incidents. Tony had told Craig he would be at Skipton at around four, so he wasn't that late. Hopefully he'd be there very soon.

Next week a satellite tracking system was being fitted in all the lorries. Pity it wasn't already up and running, as he would have been able to pin-point exactly where Tony and his unit were now.

He went back to making his coffee.

Another driver, George, arrived just as he took his first slurp, and he had to sit through chapter and verse about how the idiot of a store man in Lincoln had made him wait for no apparent reason other than that he could. Trevor made all the right noises. George always had to find something to grumble about. He was a good worker, though; he'd never had a day off sick and kept himself in trim by cycling 10 miles to work and back each day.

Trevor picked up a folder from his desk and wandered over to the counter. "How about a nice little trip to the seaside tomorrow?" he said.

George decided it sounded like a good run even though it meant an early start; he had to be at his first delivery at 9am in Winchester, before heading down to the coast and Portsmouth docks with an export order.

"It will be loaded and ready for you in the morning. Come in as early as you like."

"Thanks. Anything to pick up?"

"Nothing as yet, but give us a ring when you've finished the drop at the docks."

Trevor went back to his coffee, wishing he had remembered to get some biscuits this morning.

Andy called to say he was feeling better and asked whether there was anything available for him tomorrow, so

Trevor did a bit of shuffling and gave him the Halifax run.

He was kept busy for the next hour dealing with the drivers and didn't think of Tony again until he was about to lock up for the night. He tried ringing but it still went through to voice mail. The brewery hadn't rung again so he assumed the beer must have been delivered, and Tony was well on his way to Carlisle now. With that thought Trevor locked the door and headed home.

Helping herself to a large glass of Merlot, Susan turned on the TV and settled down to watch the news. Same old stories, just different locations. She picked up her puzzle magazine and set about trying to win a new car in the big crossword, but she couldn't concentrate on anything.

After a while John came down and announced that he had finished his homework and was off to the park to play football with his mates. Gina's friend Lucy called round and they went upstairs together to listen to music and chat about whatever eleven-year-old girls chat about.

Susan couldn't settle and wandered aimlessly around the house, straightening pictures, plumping up cushions and regularly checking that the phone was working.

She wondered whether to ring the office, but decided against it. They would think she was paranoid and tease Tony about it. She remembered the time when another driver's wife had brought his sandwiches in and one of his colleagues had seen Peppa Pig cupcakes peering through the plastic box. Although he had told them all that they were left over from his small daughter's birthday tea, his workmates ribbed him relentlessly for several weeks.

She wandered into the garden to make a start on weeding

the flower border. She grabbed her little fork, garden gloves and kneeling pad from the shed and started waging war with dandelions and red dead nettles. It was rather satisfying to see how much better it was beginning to look. The hum of a neighbour's lawnmower as it glided round was quite soothing – so much so that she nearly missed the ringing of the phone.

She raced indoors, throwing off her gloves as she went. Gina had got there before her and was chatting happily to the caller so Susan was surprised when she announced, as she handed over the phone, that rather than Tony, it was her mum's friend Julia, calling to ask if Susan would like to go to the local Food and Drink Festival in June as she could get advance tickets cheaper than on the day. She checked her diary, and told Julia to go ahead, and she would pay her back next time they met.

Bitterly disappointed that it hadn't been Tony, Susan wandered back into the garden, gathered her things together and put them back into the shed.

Lucy's mum came to collect her, and then Gina wanted to watch a nature programme about the wildlife in Australia that their geography teacher had been telling them about.

John came home and was soon playing a football game on the iPad.

Susan tried to act normally so as not to worry her children, but with little success.

"What's wrong, Mum?" asked the ever-perceptive Gina.

"Oh, nothing," Susan said, with an unconvincing laugh.

"Is it because Dad hasn't rung?"

"The signal is often bad in that area," she improvised, "and he'll be back tomorrow anyway, so we can chat then."

Gina accepted this and started chattering about the coming weekend. Susan was taking her and Lucy ice-skating in

Oxford as her birthday treat on Saturday.

"Can we have lunch at McDonald's?" she asked.

"I had thought we could go to Pizza Hut - then you and Lucy could have their ice cream that you love so much."

"That's a good idea."

That settled, Gina headed for bed to read her current library book.

"John, it's about time you packed in playing on that iPad," Susan said. "You spend far too much time on it. I do wish you would read more, like your sister."

"Reading's boring - unless it's my football magazine," he added with a little grin.

"Best you get off to bed too, my lad," she smiled as she ruffled his thick dark hair.

So like his dad, she thought, as she watched him leave the room.

She had intended to make a birthday cake for Gina, but being so distracted, she had forgotten to buy any eggs. She would pick up a ready-made one at the supermarket on the way home from work tomorrow.

With the kids now both in bed Susan got out the cards and presents for Gina and put them ready for the morning. She kept back the one from her and Tony because he would want to be able to see her open it tomorrow evening.

He would ring in the morning. He wouldn't miss wishing his daughter a happy birthday. Then she could talk to him, tell him she understood about his not wanting to go on holiday with her mother, and that she loved him.

TUESDAY 30TH APRIL

Morning

Trevor unlocked the office door and headed towards the kitchen to put the kettle on. There were already a couple of drivers chatting in the yard and the first man came in as he was sitting down with his cup of coffee, as black and strong as he could make it to wake himself up for the day. He very soon dealt with them all, and sent them on their way.

Andy wandered in a little later.

"Feeling better, mate?" asked Trevor, looking him over. "You look knackered - do you think you should be back?"

"Just feeling a bit tired. I think it was a twenty-four-hour bug."

"I've got your new work boots," Trevor told him and went to collect them. "Sign there to confirm you've received them." Once that was done, he said, "Leo's doing your Scottish run, but I've got a job from High Wycombe to Halifax for you. I just need you to take four pallets to Oxford on the way."

Andy wasn't best pleased as he was cream-crackered and had hoped that he would be on local runs today, but he put on a brave face, accepted the paperwork that Trevor handed him and wandered off to hitch the trailer to his unit.

As soon as he left, Trevor dashed to his desk, pulled out

the air freshener and liberally sprayed the office. He'd taken Andy aside some time ago and told him as kindly as he could that his BO was a problem, and suggested he take more regular baths. Things did improve for a few days, but he was smelling as high as ever now - heaven knows what he'd be like come summer. Leo had taken his own cab to Glasgow; no one wanted to use Andy's because it reeked. His colleagues called him Pongo, but never to his face. He had been with the company for about a year, having moved to the area to be with his girlfriend. The relationship hadn't lasted more than six months. Trevor thought she must have regained her sense of smell and had very soon kicked him out. He now lived in a rented flat in the rougher end of town and seemed happy enough. He did go on a bender every now and then, but not usually on a school night.

Craig arrived at 8.30 and made them both a coffee before turning on his computer and answering his first call of the day, which was from the Severn Bore Brewery.

"The beer hasn't got to Skipton yet, Trev. Did you hear from Tony at all?"

"They rang yesterday about five o'clock and I told them that Tone must've got held up. I tried to get hold of him, but his phone went to voicemail so I presumed he was driving."

Trevor speed-dialled Tony's number. Again there was no reply. Where the hell was he?

"I'm just getting the answerphone. Tell them we'll call them as soon as we can get hold of him."

Craig relayed this to the brewery, who expressed their dissatisfaction but agreed to wait for news.

"It isn't like him to turn his phone off," Trevor said. "I wonder if his wife has heard from him."

Craig looked up Tony's home number and Trevor dialled. There was no answer there, either. He glanced at the clock. "She'll have left for work. I'll try again later."

Jenny came in with a chocolate cake she had made for the boys and brought in a large slice for each of them with a cup of coffee before shutting herself away in her office to get on with the invoices.

There was a pile of messages on the fax machine. Trevor gathered them up and started working on the next day's routes while Craig manned the phone and scanned the proofs of delivery from the day before.

"Did you find any interesting holidays?" asked Trevor.

"Yes, there was a brilliant hotel in Ibiza, right by the beach, with the most amazing swimming pool. Happy hour every day and the nightlife all on the doorstep."

"Sounds great. We'll probably go to Turkey again. We really liked it last year."

"That reminds me: I need to book the last week in July and the first in August, please, Trev. Carrie can only have those two weeks off – factory fortnight."

Trevor pulled out the diary and marked Craig's holiday in. "I prefer to go in September when it's not so hot."

The brewery rang again for an update on their order and couldn't believe that the company still didn't know where their driver was.

"I'm getting really worried about Tony," Trevor admitted as he hung up.

"Do you think we ought to report him missing?"

"The police would have been in touch if he'd had an accident – the phone number is on the truck."

"True."

"It's so unlike him, not to be in touch and not to have done that delivery. He knew the beer needed to be there for the festival today."

"Perhaps he's got a woman up that way," Craig suggested. "He does go to Yorkshire every week. Plenty of chance to have met someone."

"No, I can't believe that. He seems happily married to me. They've known each other since college and he is always telling us about what they have been doing at the weekend. A family that plays together stays together."

"Well, I just can't make it out. Perhaps he's been hijacked."

"It wasn't that high value a load for anyone to want to steal it. I mean, if it were computers or electronics, then maybe, but beer? I don't think even the real ale buffs would be that desperate."

Craig accepted the sense of that with a nod. "No doubt he'll ring soon."

Jenny came out from her office and announced that everything was up to date and she would see them on Tuesday next.

"Tuesday?" queried Trevor.

"Yes, remember? I'm off to visit my mother in Weymouth tomorrow for a few days, and next Monday is a bank holiday."

"Oh, yes, of course. Have a good time. Bring us back a stick of rock," he grinned.

Gina raced into her mother's bedroom as soon as she heard the alarm start up.

"It's my birthday!"

"Happy birthday, darling," her mother hugged her. "I've got a few cards here for you."

She opened the drawer in her bedside cabinet and pulled

out half a dozen envelopes.

Gina ripped them open and was soon mentally spending the money she found inside some of them.

"I think it would be nice for you to wait until your dad comes home tonight before you open your present from us."

"Oh, all right," she agreed, with some reluctance.

"There are some other parcels for you to open downstairs, but first you have to get dressed and ready for school."

Gina didn't need telling twice. She launched herself out of the door and headed towards her own room.

Susan stretched and grabbed her dressing gown, and padded downstairs to put the kettle on to boil. She called upstairs to John that he should get up, pushed a couple of slices of bread into the toaster for him and made drinks for them all.

Presents from aunts and uncles and friends of the family were piled next to Gina's cereal bowl, where Susan had put them the night before.

Gina beat all records in getting down to the table. A new CD from Susan's sister and family, a watch from her grandmother, some chocolates from their neighbours, and a pretty butterfly pendant from her Godmother were all soon unwrapped.

"Have you bought the sweets for me to take into school, Mum?" Gina asked.

"Yes," she said, pointing to a big tub of Celebrations. "That should be enough for everyone in your class."

John came in saying he hoped there would be some left for him. He handed his sister a parcel as he sat down to butter his toast. Opening it, she found a box set of Jacqueline Wilson books.

"Fantastic! Thank you so much. These will keep me busy!" She was an avid reader and got through a book in no time at all. "I wish I didn't have to wait until tonight for my main present, but I know Dad would be really upset if he wasn't here to see me unwrap it."

As Susan cleared the table, she hoped Tony would call soon or he'd miss Gina. They had to leave for school in a few minutes. Maybe she should try to ring him again. She picked up the phone in the hall and dialled his number, but as before, after several rings it went to voice mail. She left a message and returned to the kitchen to load the dishwasher.

"Dad didn't ring to wish me happy birthday," complained Gina as she helped her mother.

"He probably still can't get a signal. I tried to phone him last night and it went to voice mail."

Susan took her daughter's cards into the living room and set them along the long shelf between family photos and ornaments. She caught sight of a picture from their holiday last year in St Ives. She really wished they hadn't fallen out so dramatically on Sunday night, and that she hadn't stormed off to bed. When he finally joined her after Match of the Day, she'd pretended to be asleep because she didn't want to speak to him. Now she wished they had cleared the air then.

Here she was worrying, and he would come waltzing through that front door tonight completely unaware of the anxiety he had caused.

John was being particularly nice to his sister for her birthday and she opened the tub of chocolates and let him choose a couple. It was a tradition at the local school to take something to share with classmates on your birthday and Gina knew they were not going to be disappointed today.

"Come on then, you two. You don't want to be late," Susan urged when they really couldn't delay any longer.

She didn't hear the phone ringing in the hall as she reversed out of the drive.

TUESDAY 30TH APRIL

Afternoon

Trevor and Craig were both enjoying the pasties which Craig had brought in from the sandwich wagon. Trevor reached for his paper and studied the form for Sandown while Craig logged onto Sports Direct, looking for some new football boots.

The brewery called again, fuming because their beer still hadn't been delivered. They had now lost the contract and wanted compensation. Trevor could only apologise, but said that until he heard from his driver, he couldn't say what the next step would be.

He tried Tony's mobile once more, and then his home number, still with no success.

He decided to check with the customer who Tony was meant to be collecting for this morning, on the off-chance.

They told him they would get in touch with the company in Cumbria to find out if the goods had been collected, and call him back.

"I can't believe this. The first time the boss goes away and leaves me in charge, a driver and his vehicle completely vanish!" he muttered as he hung up. Graham was taking a well-earned week's break, and Trevor really didn't want to bother him.

When the phone rang he snatched it up, hoping for better news; but the goods had not been picked up in Carlisle. He promised the company that he would arrange for them to be collected tomorrow by another driver who was currently in Scotland.

He called Leo. At least his phone was working, he thought, as the driver answered.

"Tony hasn't been able to pick up the backload from Carlisle. I'd like you to do it on your way down tomorrow."

Leo didn't question the change, and Trevor didn't explain; he simply gave him the details of the collection point.

The situation wasn't something he could handle on his own, though; he'd have to consult the boss. Hoping for some privacy, he went into the little office where Jenny did the accounts. Gossip spread like wildfire, and he didn't want to alarm the rest of the workforce unnecessarily.

Graham Jenkins was a self-made man who had started out as a same-day courier with a Ford Transit van, handling small removals and urgent deliveries. He found there was a demand for limited loads of palletised goods to be moved around locally and his business had grown rapidly. He now owned eight lorries and employed seven full-time drivers along with three office staff. He had bought a static caravan on the south coast on the proceeds, and he was staying there with his wife and kids when Trevor called.

"Graham, sorry to bother you, but we've, er, got a bit of a problem."

"What's wrong?" his boss demanded.

"Well, it's beginning to look like Tony's missing. He reported from his second drop yesterday in Leeds, and we haven't heard from him since. He should have gone onto Skipton from there, but they haven't seen him. He seems to have vanished completely. His phone was on voicemail yesterday, but now it's switched off."

"That's not like him at all," Graham said. "He's always been such a reliable lad."

"We haven't been able to get hold of his missus yet. Do you think I ought to ring the police?"

"Try his home again, but if you don't get any joy, you had better report it; though if there had been an accident, they'd have let you know."

"I'd have thought so. Okay, I'll try his wife again."

"Make sure you keep me informed."

"Will do." He hung up, and then tapped in Tony's home number once more.

Susan's morning had been busy. A cat had been brought in needing emergency surgery after being knocked down, which meant that everything was running late. When she finally locked up at two o'clock, she leapt into her car and drove to Morrisons to buy a birthday cake for Gina, a pretty iced sponge which she could decorate with a butterfly she had bought a few weeks ago. It would look better than it tasted, probably, but she paid and was soon heading for home.

As she was taking the cake out of the car, she could hear the house phone.

She wrestled one-handed with the front door key, haste making her clumsy, and by the time she picked up the receiver there was only the dial tone. She dialled 1471 and recognised Tony's work number.

She took the cake through into the kitchen and put it safely on the work surface before hurrying back into the hall. Gina would soon be arriving from school with her friend, who was coming for tea tonight, and Susan didn't want an audience.

"Grahams Transport."

When she gave her name, Craig told her he would put her through to his superior.

Trevor was contemplating whether to bother the police just yet when Craig came through to tell him that Mrs Hedges was on the line.

"Hello, Mrs Hedges. Thanks for calling so promptly. I was wondering if you'd heard from Tony at all today?"

"No, I haven't. In fact I am starting to get worried now. It's so unlike him not to ring me when he has a night out. It's Gina's birthday too, and he wouldn't miss that if he could help it. I thought at first that maybe he hadn't been able to get a signal. Haven't you heard from him either?"

"No, but you're probably right, and the phones are down where he is. We haven't spoken to him since yesterday lunchtime. I'm sure it's nothing serious. Chances are he'll turn up tonight and wonder what all the fuss is about. Could you tell him to call the office, if you hear from him?"

"Yes, of course. And if you hear first, can you ask him to phone me?"

"I'll do that, Mrs Hedges."

Trevor put the receiver down, wishing he felt more optimistic. He didn't want to worry her by telling her that they knew he hadn't delivered his last consignment yesterday. Tony was a genuinely nice guy and a reliable worker, who got on well with everyone. This wasn't like him at all.

"She hasn't heard from him either," he told Craig as he crossed back to his own desk. "I'm going to have to inform the police."

Between them they found the number for the local police station, and Trevor went back to sit at Jenny's desk again. He hesitated, trying to convince himself that Tony would be in touch at any moment; but there was really no alternative.

"Hello, this is Trevor Welland from Grahams Transport. I need to report a driver and vehicle missing."

WEDNESDAY 1ST MAY

Morning

Robert was up in time to hear the dawn chorus, a magical sound that started with one bird, and before long a cacophony of song filled the air.

He laced his running shoes and set off. He loved to do his training at this time of day when the lanes were free from vehicles and the countryside was just waking up.

Clad in black joggers and a long-sleeved top, he covered his fair, shoulder-length hair with a green beanie as there was still a nip in the early morning air. A mist of dew was rising from the fields as the sun started to muster its strength.

Practising for the local half marathon he had set up a Just Giving page for the nearby hospice, Oakshott House, where his younger brother had been looked after so well during his last few months.

Today he decided to take the gravel track which led upwards towards the disused limestone quarry. He had not been this way for a while and needed to get some hill practice in. He could hear the crystal-clear call of a cuckoo in the distance. It was a beautiful morning and it was good to be alive.

He pounded on past the little beech copse, with its azure carpet of bluebells, dodging the puddles which had formed recently in the potholes.

A fox ran across the road in front of him and disappeared silently into the wood as he reached the ridge, and he could hear the skylarks' shrill cries as they soared above a bright yellow oilseed rape field. He paused to listen and admire the view before carrying on towards the quarry around the next bend.

As he followed the curve of the track, he noticed an acrid smell; not the sort of thing he would associate with the countryside – more the stench you would get in an industrial town.

It wasn't long before he found the cause. As he turned the next corner, he could see the remains of a fire further along the track; and drawing closer, he thought it might be a vehicle of some sort which had come to grief. Perhaps it was a plane. Would he be able to get past it? He slowed down to a gentler pace.

The smell became worse the closer he got, and he started to cough. Taking his hat off and holding it in front of his nose and mouth he edged nearer to what must have been a lorry, although it looked like there had been an explosion as there were parts scattered all around. The fumes made his eyes run, and he tripped over a piece of debris, falling and grazing his knee. Directly in front of him, he was horrified to see a severed finger lying on the road.

He leapt up and raced back down the track in total shock. After about a hundred yards he stopped, dragged out his mobile phone and jabbed in 112. He was shaking uncontrollably and was barely able to speak.

Robert asked for the police and with difficulty explained to the emergency call centre where he was and what he had found. They told him to sit down and take deep breaths, and to stay where he was as they would send someone out.

He sank down on the grass verge and waited for them to arrive. Still shivering with shock, he couldn't get the vision of what he had seen out of his head. Usually he would have enjoyed the fantastic view down to his village and far beyond, but today he was numb to all of it.

First to arrive on the scene was a police patrol car. The driver walked up to view the site while his colleague came over to Robert and invited him to sit in the car, explaining that he needed to take down some information.

Shortly afterwards a Ford Focus drew up and a couple of plain-clothed men got out. The younger and taller of the two set off up the track to speak to the uniformed officer who was on his way down to meet him.

"Bit of a mess, sir. Looks like there has been an explosion. At least one casualty."

The tall man pulled out his phone and summoned forensics and a fire investigation team, while the shorter one introduced himself to Robert as DCI Cooke and asked the patrolman if he had finished his questions.

All Robert could think of was that he needed to get to work soon. "I'll be late," he said. "They won't like it."

"You've had a nasty shock, lad. My officer here will take you home. I'll drop by to see you later; what time do you finish work?"

"Six o' clock."

"I'll come by about seven, then," Cooke told him as he walked over to join the other two.

Trevor had been in a meeting with PC Smith for about an hour this morning and wasn't in the best of moods when he returned to the main office.

"I don't think the constable was very impressed that

couldn't tell him the address that Tony was delivering to in Leeds," he barked at his junior colleague. "You really need to pay more attention to detail!"

"It was such a rush, there were drivers coming in and I had to let the boys in the yard know to leave a space for the extra pallet," Craig replied defensively.

"They wanted to know if there was anything of high value on the load. I told them it was only ceramic tiles for a new housing development, which had already been delivered, the beer from the artisan microbrewery in the forest, which was going to the Real Ale Festival in Skipton, and the chemical - what chemical was it?"

"I didn't ask. He was going to give all the paperwork to Tony," Craig bleated.

"Half a job, Craig, half a job!" his manager shouted. Then, after some thought, he asked, "Did Tony seem okay to you on Monday morning?"

"A bit pissed off about the extra drop, but otherwise he seemed fine. Why?"

"The officer asked if he had seemed worried or depressed lately. I thought he was all right and told him that he had been his cheerful self on Friday when I saw him last."

"They don't think that he's done something stupid, do they? What are they going to do now?"

"Their next port of call will be Cotswold Chemicals, to get the Leeds address. We know he arrived there, so it's where he went from there that is the mystery. They told his missus last night that he and his unit were officially missing. Poor lass will be beside herself – and with two kiddies, too."

"It just doesn't make sense. People don't just vanish." Craig shook his head as he wandered into the kitchen to make them both a coffee. Being the office junior, drinks-making was his job.

"I'd better go and phone Graham and keep him up to date," Trevor stated as he headed for the privacy of Jenny's office and shut the door.

When he returned, he announced that he had managed to stop their boss from cutting short his well-earned break, telling him that the matter was now in the hands of the police and that he would keep him informed.

A horn blasted in the yard, announcing the arrival of the catering wagon, and Craig got to his feet. "Do you want anything today?" he asked.

"No thanks, mate. I've got some left-over casserole from last night to stick in the microwave."

Craig went off and came back with a bacon roll smothered in tomato ketchup, which he quickly devoured, but not without dripping the red sauce over the paperwork on his desk.

Trevor took the plastic box of leftovers out of the fridge in the cubby-hole kitchen and set it to heat through in the microwave. He mopped up the mess that Craig had made earlier while grumbling to himself as he waited for the welcome 'ping'.

Once lunch was over, the office returned to its normal routine with Craig taking calls from customers and logging them onto the computer and Trevor making up loads for the next day.

Leo rang to say he had picked up from Carlisle, and that he probably wouldn't be back until the next morning.

The mood in the office turned sombre as time went on, and both colleagues worried about their driver.

"I've got some biscuits in my drawer to go with our tea this afternoon," Trevor hinted.

"I'll go and get the drinks then."

"Make sure you don't say anything to the other drivers about Tony," the manager reminded him as his mug of tea arrived. "They'll find out soon enough, but hopefully he will be back by then and able to tell the tale himself."

In an effort to lighten the air Craig announced that he had found a holiday and they were going to book it on Saturday.

"Where are you going? That place in Ibiza?"

"Yes. Es Cana. It's half board and really near the beach. Got a swimming pool with a bar, games room and a full activities agenda so we shouldn't get bored," Craig enthused, "and we can fly from Birmingham, which is so much more convenient."

"Sounds great," said Trevor, thinking he preferred his all-inclusive in Turkey. Beer and snacks available all day at the pool bar and a chance to relax – that was what he wanted from a holiday.

Some time later Trevor took a call from the local police.

"Craig, your incompetence strikes again! The police have been out to Bullnose Farm, and guess what? No-one there has heard of Cotswold Chemicals."

"Well, he definitely did the pickup, because he rang to complain that it needed the tail lift, and I had asked the boys to leave a space behind the first drop. So it's not me being incompetent," he said, hackles rising. "He couldn't pick up if there was no company to pick up from, could he?"

WEDNESDAY 1ST MAY

Afternoon

DCI Ben Cooke was eating a sandwich, and watching the world go by from his first-floor office window, when he received the call from his team at the vehicle fire site. They had found a number plate in the wreckage with which, if it was legitimate, he could now find out who was the registered owner. That was a good start. Maybe they could then identify the victim. He took down the registration number and gave it to Sharon, his DI.

"Can you go and run this through the computer, love? We might be getting nearer to finding out who that poor devil is in the burnt-out truck."

Sharon hated being called 'love'; it was so patronising. She sighed as she took the scrap of paper off him.

Generally he wasn't a bad boss and was always first in the chair when the department went out for a well-earned drink; but he would insist on calling all the female officers 'love'.

She soon came back with the information

"The truck is registered to Grahams Transport in Gloucestershire," she announced. "Shall I get on to their local force to go and have a word with them?"

"No, I'll ring them first and let them know. Have you got their number there?"

Sharon read it out, and he made a note.

"Apparently the fire started in the freight part of the vehicle and seems to have been caused by an explosion of some sort. I wonder what he was carrying," he said as he dialled. He was soon put through to the transport manager.

"Mr Welland? This is DCI Cooke from Derbyshire Constabulary," he started. "I understand you are the registered owner of a DAF truck, registration number GT63 ABD. Can you confirm that to me? You can? I'm afraid it has been found burnt out in our area."

Sharon went off to get a couple of coffees from the vending machine while her boss explained about the vehicle and the burnt body therein.

When she returned, he was just finishing off his conversation, and she waited for him to end the call.

"Thanks, love," he said at the sight of the plastic cup arriving on his desk. "Sounds like the vehicle has been missing since Monday afternoon. The last time they spoke to the driver was at lunch time, when he rang in from a drop in Leeds where he was delivering a pallet of hazardous goods. His next delivery was due to be to a beer festival in Skipton later in the afternoon but he never arrived there. They reported it to their local police yesterday when they still couldn't contact him and he failed to turn up at his scheduled collection point. The driver was a Tony Hedges; been with the company for some years."

"So was he carrying anything hazardous?"

"No. He did have a pallet of hazardous material, but that was his Leeds delivery. His company told me that he would have only had his last load, which was beer."

"So how did he end up on our patch?"

"They have no idea. It's a real mystery. He left on a regular route to Yorkshire on Monday and should have arrived in Cumbria later in the day to collect a load to go back to Gloucestershire."

"Perhaps he was on a foreigner - doing a bit of work on the side."

"It's a possibility, certainly something we will have to keep in mind," replied her boss as he got up from his chair to look out of the window. "I'm going to see the young lad who found the wreck this evening. Maybe he's seen the truck previously."

"Do you want me to ring Gloucestershire to let them know we've found it?"

"Yes, please, love. Ask them to find out the driver's blood group, and also if they can get something with DNA or fingerprints so we can see if there's a match with the finger. The body's burnt beyond recognition."

"On it, sir," she said with a mock salute.

He took it in good part. They had an easy-going relationship; she was a good detective and he was pleased to have her on his team.

Cooke yawned. It had been an early start. He hadn't had time to have a shave and he was feeling decidedly unkempt. There wasn't much he could do until the morning when there might be more information from the site and from the lab. It seemed like it might have been an unfortunate accident, but even if that was the case, he wanted to know more about why the driver had ended up at a disused quarry here in Derbyshire. He decided to knock off and go home for a hot shower and much-needed shave. He had arranged to go and speak to the lad at 7pm so didn't feel guilty about the early finish.

Craig had stopped what he was doing and had been listening avidly to the one-sided conversation that had taken place after he had put the police through to his manager.

The colour had drained from Trevor's cheeks as he thanked the person on the other end of the line.

"Have they found Tony?" Craig asked, as Trevor put the receiver down.

"I'm afraid they have found what is probably the remains of his unit near Matlock, in Derbyshire, of all places. There are human remains, but at this point they can't say whose."

"What the hell was he doing there? He was meant to be in Yorkshire!"

"Dunno, mate. I'd better go and ring Graham." He got up tiredly, and went to shut himself away in Jenny's office.

Craig just sat in stunned silence.

"Graham's coming back tonight," Trevor announced as he returned to his desk. It wasn't surprising, as the boss had always regarded the workforce as his extended family. "He wants to go and see Tony's wife, and he said he should be the one to tell the workforce – so keep it to yourself, okay?"

Craig nodded dumbly.

After a while the drivers started to arrive back in the yard, bringing their paperwork along with their trials and tribulations of the day.

A call came in from one driver who had run out of diesel 15 miles from base, so they had to get a mechanic to go out to rescue him. At least this trivial matter helped to keep the two colleagues' minds off the tragic news.

Pongo would be out for the night, having got held up on his trip to Halifax, so Trevor gave him a collection from Tamworth to make on his way back the next day.

Craig left at about five o'clock as Wednesday evening was football training. Trevor thought it would do him good to get out in the fresh air.

Another driver, Paul, wasn't at all impressed with a new warehouse man. "He made me wait while he finished his cup of tea, and didn't even offer me one," he complained. "Made me late for my last pickup, and believe me, the guy there wasn't best pleased as he was wanting to lock up."

Only when he paused for breath did he notice how drawn Trevor was looking.

"You all right, mate?"

"Just a bit of a headache," Trevor lied.

It was time to lock up for the day and he headed out to the yard.

He waved to the two forklift drivers who were busy unloading collections and putting them onto vehicles for delivery the next day or into the warehouse for a later one.

"Everything okay?" he shouted.

"Yes, fine, thanks," replied the more senior of the two.

"Make sure you lock up before you leave," he said. Then, satisfied, he climbed into his car and headed home, safe in the knowledge that at least everything would be ready for the drivers in the morning.

WEDNESDAY 1ST MAY

Evening

The church clock was striking seven when DCI Cooke knocked at 11 Laverton Avenue.

It was raining and he was sheltering under the porch when the door opened a crack. Cooke showed his warrant card and was admitted into the bright hallway by a trim middle-aged woman.

"We were expecting you," she smiled nervously, showing him into the cosy living room. "Poor Robert – such a shock. I'll just go and fetch him for you."

"Thanks. I won't keep him long."

The mantle clock ticked loudly and Cooke took the room in as he waited. A large ornate brass mirror hung above the fireplace where a flower arrangement stood in front of a black mesh fire screen. Either the open fire was obsolete now or wasn't expected to be needed again until next winter. A small modern CD player stood on an old-fashioned oak sideboard amid photos of various family members, judging from the facial similarities. The television was on standby, probably switched off quickly when he knocked. Rain hit the net-curtained bay window which looked out onto the street.

Robert came in wiping oily hands on a piece of rag.

"Hello, lad. You are looking a better colour now. I'd like to ask you a few questions, if that's all right?'"

Robert nodded, and sat down on the dark blue sofa with his hands resting on the knees of his grubby jeans. Cooke took the armchair opposite.

"Do you go out running every day?"

"I have been since I started training for the local half marathon."

"And do you take the same route every day?"

"No, I like to vary it. That route gives me some practice for the hillier parts of the race, but I haven't been that way for a few weeks."

"Have you ever seen a truck out there before?"

"No; I usually don't see anyone at all. It's really peaceful at that time in the morning."

"So you have never met anyone or seen any other vehicles while running up that particular track?"

"No, like I say, there's nobody else around that early. I see plenty of wildlife, but I've never met anyone. Since the quarry closed some years ago the track is a dead end, and I have to run through fields after I pass the lake."

"No other runners, or walkers?"

"No, although others probably use the route later in the day."

"Have you mentioned that route to anyone? Work colleagues, friends?"

"I don't think so. I always run alone, and the lads at work take the piss out of me – they'd rather be down the pub than keeping fit."

Cooke took a card from his inside pocket and passed it over.

"Here's my number. Give me a call if you remember seeing anyone up there at any time, okay?"

Robert nodded, took the card and rose to put it on the mantelpiece behind the carriage clock.

Cooke left the house and walked back to his car, hoping that Robert would remember something that would give him a clue. He thought that former quarry workers and their drivers would know about the track; and although the ordinary dog walkers of the village would probably not like the steep climbs, serious hikers would enjoy the views that the place offered.

Before heading home, he called his wife. His was rarely a nine to five job, and after too many dried up dinners, they had decided that she wouldn't bother to cook for him until she knew he was actually en route.

"Hi, love, I'm heading home now."

"You know I'm out tonight? It's the first Wednesday of the month so I'm off to Flower Club in a couple of minutes."

He groaned; he had forgotten.

"There's a pepperoni pizza in the freezer, it won't take many minutes to warm that through and there is plenty of salad in the fridge that you can have with it."

Deep joy, he thought, but said, "Great. See you later then."

She knew he wasn't impressed. He didn't like having to get his own dinner, but it was only once a month and it wouldn't hurt him.

"I made a coffee and walnut cake while I was baking one for the ladies, so you can have a slice of that for afters."

That raised his spirits. "Thanks," he replied, a little more enthusiastically.

Deciding to take the scenic route home, he slotted Coldplay's A Head Full of Dreams album into the player, turned up the volume and sang along with Chris Martin to the title track.

THURSDAY 2ND MAY

Morning

The mid-morning sun was filtering through the branches of the mighty oak tree which stood guard over the police station and cast a shimmering shadow onto the paperwork on Ben Cooke's desk. He was already on his second caffeine fix of the day when the harsh ringing of his phone disturbed him from his perusal of the menu from Lettuce Eat, the new deli in Market Street.

"I'm on my way back from the quarry," Sharon informed him. "They've found part of an arm with a distinctive tattoo so we should be able to identify the victim. It must have been one hell of an explosion, because it was quite a distance from the main wreckage."

Cooke shuffled through the papers in the file on the burnt-out vehicle and found the driver's photograph. He was wearing a long-sleeved rugby shirt.

"I'll need to have a photo of that tattoo so that I can send it through for identification."

"Already on it," she told him. "Forensics will forward it this afternoon once they've been able to clean the arm up and get a good picture of it."

"Good. I'll keep an eye out for it."

He chose a bacon, brie and cranberry baguette from the

menu, put the photo of the driver back into the file and strolled down to the general office where the lunch order was being compiled.

Sharon caught up with him when she got back an hour later.

"What do you think the truck was doing here on our patch?" Cooke asked.

"Maybe it was a lovers' tryst and the husband found out," suggested Sharon, not altogether seriously.

"Could be, but they have only found one body. We can't rule out a suicide."

"Possible. It's a quiet spot, well out of the way. Or perhaps someone had told him about it as a good place to park up for the night for free."

"Unlikely. From the notes we have, the driver did the same run every week up to Yorkshire, and he always had a collection from Cumbria so would spend the night up that way."

"We need to find out more about him. Did he have a bit on the side who he would meet when he was up this way? Has he any other connections with Yorkshire or Derbyshire? Does he have a record?"

"Go and find Jimmy - see what he can dig up on him."

"Will do, guv."

He returned to his office and dialled through to Gloucestershire to let them know about the new find. He would send through the photo later for them to show to Mrs Hedges for a possible identification.

On her way to see him, Sharon literally bumped into James Weeks, a decidedly overweight colleague who was more interested in the greasy butty he was eating than his surroundings.

"Look where you're going!" she cried as the papers she was carrying flew out of her hand and across the corridor.

"Sorry, mate," Weeks mumbled, as he wiped the grease from round his mouth with the back of his hand.

Sharon quickly picked up her papers to stop her colleague from touching them. He was a slob, and not one of Sharon's favourite people on the team, but he was a whizz-kid on the computer and a necessary cog in the workforce machine.

"We need to find some info on Tony Hedges, a lorry driver from Gloucestershire; aged forty-two; works for Grahams Transport. See if he's on our files anywhere. In particular, we want to know if he has any links with this area."

Jimmy confirmed he would get onto it, and she hurried away, keen to escape the unpleasant fried-food odour that always seemed to linger after he'd gone.

THURSDAY 2ND MAY

Late afternoon

WPC Christine Shilton locked up the car and walked slowly towards the three-bedroomed semi belonging to the Hedges family. It was just a matter of showing Mrs Hedges the photo she had slipped into an envelope before leaving the station so that she could confirm, or otherwise, the identity of the deceased.

She took in the neat borders in the front garden as she walked up the path. It was a warm afternoon and the scent of wallflowers filled the air, taking her back to her childhood when her father had always planted them on the edge of his small vegetable patch. She knocked at the blue UPVc door and waited, watching for movement through the blue and green patterned glass panel.

Susan appeared, red eyed, and Shilton thought, from the look of her, that she had probably not slept a wink since the visit from the police yesterday.

Seeing the uniform, Susan opened the door fully, and walked trance-like through to the kitchen, leaving the WPC to follow her.

"I didn't even get to say goodbye," was all she said as she sank onto a wooden dining chair.

"Mrs Hedges, we have a photograph we would like you to look at so that we can verify whether or not the person found was your husband," Shilton explained, taking a seat on the opposite side of the kitchen table.

Susan took the photo from her and made herself look at it.

"Do you recognise the tattoo in the picture?"

Susan frowned and shook her head. "I have never seen it before."

Shilton hid her surprise. This had seemed such an open and shut case as far as the identity of the victim was concerned.

"Then either someone else was with your husband when this happened or he wasn't in the vehicle at the time. Does he have any family or friends in Derbyshire?"

"No. Certainly no-one I know of."

"Can you think of any reason why he would have gone to Derbyshire when he was meant to be in Yorkshire?"

"None whatsoever." Susan's brain was racing. "Could this mean that Tony is alive after all?"

Before the constable could respond, there was the sound of a key in the front door and Susan raced out to the hallway.

It was her mother with a pair of very subdued children behind her.

"Did you manage to get any sleep?" she asked her daughter, before spotting the police officer. "We've been for a long walk across the fields," she explained. "I thought Sue might have more chance of a rest."

Susan shook her head. "It might not have been Tony," she told her mother excitedly as they all followed her into the kitchen.

"But they said it was his vehicle."

"I know, it's really odd. Maybe someone stole it." A worried look darkened her face again. "But we still don't know where he is," she said, resuming her seat.

"We may need to come back and speak to you again," Shilton said. "If you can think of anyone he might have known up that way in the meantime, or anything that you consider might be helpful, please let us know."

The constable took out her notebook, wrote down the phone number and the name of her immediate superior, tore the page out and gave it to her.

Susan took the slip of paper, completely lost in thought.

Shilton didn't like to say anything at this stage, but it was looking as if Tony, far from being a victim, was now more likely to be a suspect.

As she left the room, she saw that Gina and John had hurried over to where their mother was still sitting and were giving her a big hug. Whichever way it went, she was going to need all the support that they and their grandmother could give.

If Tony wasn't in that lorry, where is he? And who was the owner of the tattoo?

Once in her car she used her mobile to report back to base so that they could inform Derbyshire of the new turn of events.

FRIDAY 3RD MAY

Morning

Sharon had already typed up a brief summary and was handing it out to her colleagues when DCI Cooke entered the open-plan office carrying a much-needed black coffee. He hadn't slept very well and had just come off a phone call with Gloucestershire's finest.

"This was only going to be a brief meeting when I called it yesterday, to bring you up to scratch on the incident at the quarry earlier this week. Things, however, have now moved on."

He walked over to the board and pointed at the photograph of the wreckage.

"This lorry, which we know belongs to Grahams Transport, a haulage company in Gloucestershire, was found burnt out at the old quarry near the village of Wellsend yesterday. One person, who we at first believed to be the driver, Tony Hedges, perished in the blaze."

Sharon gave him a quizzical look which he acknowledged but carried on.

"I have just been speaking to the fire team and they tell me that it originated with a chemical explosion in the back of the vehicle sometime on Monday night. Part of an arm was found nearby bearing a distinctive tattoo, and we sent an image of it through to Gloucestershire in order to try to get a positive ID on the victim."

He looked around the room before dealing the next card.

"I have just been speaking to WPC Shilton from

Gloucestershire Police. She says that Tony Hedges' wife has told her the tattoo did not belong to him."

Sharon straightened.

He stuck the photo of the tattoo onto the white board, and wrote 'Unknown Victim' below it.

"What we have here is an unexplained death of an unknown person. We don't know whether he died where he was found or elsewhere and moved there, possibly in the vehicle. It also means that the driver, Hedges, who is still unaccounted for, has now become a person of interest."

"Tony Hedges —" he pointed again to the photo " — should have been delivering beer in Yorkshire. So what was he doing in Derbyshire? He does a regular run every week: what was his usual routine?"

"Does he have any friends or relatives round here?" asked DS Tom Golding.

"His wife says not, so our victim could be someone he met in Yorkshire while working as he goes there every week." Cooke looked at Jimmy. "Have you been able to find anything in our records about him? Does he have any form?"

"Not a thing. Squeaky clean, not even a parking fine."

"When was he last seen?" asked Milner, the constable who, with his colleague Truman, had been first on the scene.

"His company heard from him at lunchtime on Monday to say he had got to the delivery point, which we know was near Leeds. That's all the information we have about that. He was given the delivery address at the collection point, a company called Cotswold Chemicals, which has mysteriously vanished."

"That sounds dodgy to me," piped up DS Golding.

"Yes, Tom, I thought the same," replied the DCI, "but we have to keep an open mind. Tony Hedges may be behind a fictitious delivery. We need to find him. Any questions?

He looked round at the team. No one spoke.

"Okay, Jimmy, the quarry is closed now, but could you find out who used to own it and whether they still have a list of the personnel who worked there?"

Jimmy noted this down.

"Also can you alert the press and put the tattoo photo onto social media? We need to find out who the poor devil was." He handed him a copy. "As you can see, the image is of a dog of some sort."

Weeks took the photo and looked at it.

"It looks more like a fox to me. I'll scan it and send it out digitally."

"Tom, find out what cameras there are between Leeds and Wellsend, which might have picked up the vehicle en route. The previous drop was in Sheffield; the information is in the notes. Have a word with the people there and find out what the driver was like when he delivered. Was he edgy, distracted, maybe?"

"Milner, you and Truman drive out to the village near the quarry track this afternoon and ask any dog walkers or joggers if they've seen anyone new while they have been out and about. A vehicle they didn't recognise parked up, anything out of the ordinary. Take some copies of Hedges' photo; see if anyone recognises him. Take photos of the tattoo as well – our victim could have been local."

Off you go then, all of you. Any information, however small, report back to me or Sharon immediately. Sharon, can you meet me in my office in thirty minutes?"

He left the room with his now cold coffee, and the team resumed their work.

He climbed the stairs hoping that the reports he had requested had been sent through from Gloucestershire. He needed to get a better idea of the man they were looking for.

"Okay, guv?" Sharon asked as she entered the office a little later.

"Something about this isn't right," he said. "Family man, good worker, liked by his colleagues; Tony Hedges is a general all-round good guy. But he is missing from his vehicle, and so far, he is our only suspect."

"Maybe something happened which clicked a switch and caused him to lose control."

"Seems more pre-meditated to me."

"The sooner we find out who the body is, the sooner we can start looking for a motive."

"I think I need to go south and have a word with the people who know him – find out more about him. As it's Friday, most if not all of the drivers will be back for the bank holiday weekend, so I need to go today. Can you phone Grahams and ask them to arrange for the staff to come and speak with me as they arrive back to base? I'll leave in fifteen minutes – may as well speak to the office staff first."

FRIDAY 3RD MAY

Late afternoon

It had taken three hours, with a short stop for a sandwich and a coke at a service station near Warwick, to drive down to the scenic Cotswold village where Grahams Transport were based.

He introduced himself to the short, sandy-haired man who came to greet him as he approached the counter.

"Trevor Welland. I'm the Transport Manager," the man said. "Come this way."

A younger man raised his hand in nervous greeting as they passed his desk

"Can I get you a drink?" Trevor asked as he showed his visitor through into Jenny's office.

"A black coffee would be good," Cooke replied as he took a seat at the neat desk and put his briefcase on the floor beside him.

He bent down and took out a folder which he placed on the desk in front of him, and waited for Trevor to return.

The coffee arrived in a mug with a Union Jack design. Cooke was pleased to see that it wasn't in a plastic cup from a vending machine.

"Are you free to have a chat first?" he asked the manager.

"Yes, Craig can man the fort for the time being."

Cooke took his Parker pen from the inside pocket of his jacket.

"Will the owner be in today?"

"Yes, he is travelling up from his caravan on the south coast this afternoon. Should be here soon."

"I'm just trying to get an idea about what sort of chap Tony Hedges is," Cooke stated. "I've been told that he's a good worker, but what's he like as a person?"

"A really pleasant guy. He is married with two little 'uns and always speaks well of them all. A lot of the lads meet up at the Red Lion on a Friday night and he usually goes, but they say he doesn't stay that long. This," he waved a hand to indicate all that had happened, "is just so out of character.

Cooke was making notes. "Did he seem different lately? What was his mood like on Monday?"

"The last time I saw him was last Friday, and he seemed his normal self. Craig was on early on Monday, and he would have said if anything was off. You can ask him yourself."

"Can you compile a list of all your employees and where they were on that day?" asked Cooke, thinking it would useful to have their whereabouts to hand when he spoke to them later. Furthermore, he would get more about the character of the man from the pals he had a drink with.

"I'll go and print it off." Trevor got up to leave. "That's if you have finished with me?"

"Yes, I think so, for now."

Craig was next in the hot seat.

"Hello, Craig." Cooke took in the fact that the boy looked terrified.

"Hello." Craig sat down, gripping his hands in his lap.

"I believe it was you who took the call from –" he looked at his notes "– Cotswold Chemicals?"

"Yes, I did." Craig looked as if he was going to burst into tears so Cooke decided not to admonish him as he had probably been given a severe bollocking already.

"What can you tell me about the person who rang?"

"It was a man. I don't think he gave me his name."

"Did you recognise his voice? Was it, maybe, someone who may have worked here or for a company you have dealings with?"

"No, I didn't know him."

"Did he have an accent? Was he local, do you think?"

"I don't know. I can't remember."

"Think about it and if anything comes to you, let me know." Cooke handed him his card.

"Now, from what I understand, the man didn't tell you what the goods were, or the address they were going to."

"It was really busy, and I didn't ask." Craig was near to tears again. "I told him how much it would cost to deliver to Leeds, and he said he would give the necessary paperwork and money to the driver."

"It was definitely Leeds the load was to go to?"

"Yes."

"Okay, that's all for now. Where's the toilet?"

Craig pointed to the door in the corner of the main office and went back to his desk.

A few minutes later, Cooke returned to the little office and found the list that Trevor had promised sitting next to another mug of coffee.

Before he had time to read it, Graham Jenkins arrived and, after a quick word with Trevor, came through to see Cooke.

He introduced himself as he held out his hand to the DCI. "I know you would like to speak to me, but you'll understand that

I really want to tell the lads myself about Tony's disappearance. The first one is due back any minute."

Shaking his hand, Cooke agreed, and asked him to send each one through to him once he had spoken to them. With a grateful nod, Graham hurried across the main area to his well-lit glass-screened office.

Cooke looked at the list: Glasgow; off sick; Lincoln; Local; London; on loan to Crafted Stone Supplies. Nothing popped out at him.

The first driver back was Leo, who was visibly shaken by the news he had just been given. He had been in Glasgow by Monday night. He had spoken to Tony on Monday morning. Tony had told him about the extra drop in Leeds and agreed to meet up at the Red Lion on Friday evening as usual.

Next was Andy, who according to the list was off sick on Monday. He told Cooke that he thought it had been a twenty-four-hour bug and had been back at work on Tuesday. Cooke noticed he had a northern accent and asked him how long he had been living down south. He said he'd been with the company for about a year.

After he left, Trevor popped in with a can of air freshener, for which Cooke was very grateful.

George had taken a full load of horse feed to a retail company in Lincoln. He was back Monday night.

Paul was in the seven-and-a half tonner doing local deliveries and pickups. He had tried ringing Tony on Tuesday about a skittles match but had not been able to get through, so had decided to speak to him about it on Friday.

The next driver was away in London all morning and did a local collection in the afternoon; and the last had been out on loan to the quarry up the road, delivering their stone locally.

All the men said the same: Tony Hedges was the salt of the earth, a really good-natured guy.

Lastly Graham Jenkins entered the office.

"I'll try not to keep you long, Mr Jenkins." Cooke noticed how drained he looked. "Can you tell me how long Mr Hedges has worked for you?"

"He has been with me for about twelve years. He was the first driver I employed when I realised I could no longer do all the driving myself."

"All his colleagues speak highly of him. He's obviously a good worker, but what do you think of him as a man?"

"He is always smart and takes a pride in his appearance – that's something I first noticed at his interview. He's polite and trustworthy and takes good care of his truck. He always has a smile on his face."

"Where did he work before he came to you?"

"He had spent some years at Cirencester Agricultural College, where he met his wife, and was working for a large farm locally. He loves animals and really enjoyed his job but with one kiddy and another on the way they were struggling for cash, so he needed a career change."

"Did the job here offer him promotion prospects?"

"Yes. He passed his test for Class Two and now drives an 18 tonner. We are going to get him trained for Class One so he will be able to drive an artic too."

By now it was 7.30 and Cooke didn't fancy the long drive home. Jenkins suggested a couple of establishments which should have rooms at this time of the year.

Cooke thanked him for his and his staff's assistance, and walked out to his car. He phoned his wife and told her he would drive back up early tomorrow, and then headed down into the village centre, parked in the market square and headed towards

The Crown Inn which had boards outside advertising 'Good Food' and 'Vacant Rooms'.

SATURDAY 4TH MAY

Morning

DCI Cooke skipped breakfast and made an early start for home. It was Saturday morning, and with very little to go on he would be able to enjoy the weekend with his wife. He stopped en route to phone her to ask if she fancied a trip out with their dog when he got back. They could have a bite to eat somewhere too. She readily agreed as that meant she wouldn't have to cook later.

When he arrived just before noon, Alice suggested taking her little Corsa, as he had already driven enough for one day. She knew that a spot of lunch was likely to be in a pub and as she didn't drink, she was always happy to drive.

Cooke, with his copper's head on, suggested they go up to Wellsend, as he wanted to take another look at the disused limestone quarry where the burnt-out lorry had been found earlier in the week. It would be a great spot to walk with the dog and he could get a feel for the place at the same time.

They parked up in the village and soon reached the place where the track began, and started to take the route which young Robert would have used on his morning run. The sun was shining in a forget-me-not blue sky and the skylarks were soaring high above their nests like little dots, hardly visible, their crisp song filling the air. Cowslips were blooming on the side of the track, and Buster ran off ahead, stopping to sniff and scent-mark as he went.

Cooke stopped to look down on the village below.

"I wonder if the victim was from there," Alice said.

"It's certainly possible, but we haven't had any reports of anyone missing."

"I suppose it's a sign of the times that no one has yet noticed that a neighbour hasn't been around for a few days. Back when we were younger everyone knew everyone and what they were doing."

"True."

They climbed further up the gravel track until they saw the police tape signifying the wreckage site some two hundred metres ahead. Cooke called Buster back and put him on his lead before he could stray into the protected area.

"What a mess!" Alice exclaimed as they drew nearer. "It ruins the wonderful view."

"It certainly does." Cooke agreed.

He recognised the officer on duty as PCSO Marlow, who had only joined them recently. "Stay here with the dog," he advised Alice. " I'll just go and have a word."

As he approached he took out his ID, in case the newbie did not remember him.

"Good morning, sir," the PCSO said as he inspected the ID.

"Marlow, isn't it?"

"Yes, sir."

"Do you know if our investigators have found any more body parts?"

"I don't think so, sir. They think that most of the body burned where it was. They are still sifting through everything and say that it will still take some time as the debris is spread over such a wide area. You only just missed them, as they have gone to get some lunch."

"Have you seen anyone up here apart from our men?"

"A few dog walkers, like yourselves, but I soon sent them on their way."

"Good work, lad." Cooke walked back to where Alice was waiting.

"We'll have to double back," he said. "There's a nice-looking pub in the village claiming to serve 'Good Grub'. We might be able to have a reasonable spot of lunch there."

"That sounds like a very good idea," Alice replied and they all headed back to the car.

They soon found the pub, and parked up outside a window so that they could keep an eye on the dog if they weren't allowed to take him in with them.

It was a pretty place, with a magnificent wisteria which practically covered the front wall of the building with its pendulous lilac blooms. Inside, they found a spacious but cosy lounge bar. South facing, it was enjoying the best of the sunshine and there was a low murmur of conversation from the several couples already there. They were able to secure a square wooden table with a comfortable window seat overlooking the car park. Salt and pepper pots sat where years ago an ash tray would have been, and between them was propped a menu which offered a good selection of lunches. Cooke had noticed a blackboard next to the bar offering specials of the day, where he had seen Homemade Steak & Mushroom Pie, and decided to go for that while Alice, who was much more figure-conscious, opted for grilled chicken with salad and new potatoes.

Cooke made his way to where the landlord was talking to a couple of men who he took to be locals, seated on bar stools. He ordered the food along with a pint of Dancing Duck bitter and a diet cola for Alice.

"Nice little pub you've got here," he remarked as his pint was being pulled. "Quite busy, too, I should think."

"Aye. We attract quite a lot of walkers from Easter right through to Autumn, and the locals like to be able to walk to their watering hole, so we stay busy during the winter months too."

"Do you mind if we bring our dog in? He'll sit quietly under the table."

"Of course you can. I don't mind as long as he's well behaved."

Cooke took the drinks back to the table.

"I'm just going to fetch Buster," he told Alice. "The landlord says it's okay."

As they ate, they could hear that the talk at the bar had changed to the mystery of the burnt-out vehicle up at the quarry, and Cooke was eager to join in their discussion; so as soon as he had devoured the last of his pie he asked Alice if she'd like another drink.

"Same again?" enquired the landlord.

"Yes, please. This dog-walking is thirsty work."

"Oh, where have you been?"

"Up a track, just outside the village. Some beautiful views from up there."

"Aye, there are that. I used to drive up there every day. Worked for the quarry back along, before it shut down. I was lucky to get redundancy; the tenancy on this place came up and I've been here ever since."

Cooke decided it was time to ask some questions and showed his card to the landlord.

"I couldn't help hearing you talking about the accident up near the quarry."

"Aye, I was just discussing it with Bill and Harry here. It's a bit of a mystery why anyone would drive up there. It's not renowned for being a lovers' lane - too bumpy, not the sort of place you'd want to take your car."

Cooke had thought the same when he had driven up there earlier in the week.

"Young Robert Mills found it the other morning while out running, must have been one hell of a shock for the poor lad," Harry added as he shook his head. "I was talking to his dad last night and he told me that Robert had said the vehicle had been blown to kingdom come. He found a finger, just imagine that, so there must have been someone in it."

"You mentioned walkers. Is that track on the local walking routes?"

"No, there has never been an adopted footpath going up there, so they wouldn't have it on their maps as a right of way."

Cooke turned to the landlord. "Have you noticed anyone missing from the normal clientele?"

He shook his head, but Bill, eager to get in on the action, pointed out, "A lot of the young ones don't come in 'til the weekend with working during the week. We used to have a darts team but the league packed up some years ago. No one came forward to run it. It's the likes of old codgers like us that keep Ron here busy."

"Come to think of it, the missus woke me the other night to tell me she had heard a loud noise," Harry remembered. "We listened for a while and it was silent so I told her she must have imagined it. Bloody nuisance, as I couldn't get back to sleep for ages afterwards."

"Any idea what time that was?"

"It must have been after two as I heard the church clock strike three."

"That's very helpful, sir, thank you.."

He took the two glasses and returned to sit with his wife.

"Not the sort of place that the local lovers would frequent due to the potholes," he told her as he took a swig from his glass. "The landlord keeps a good pint, I must say," he added, "and this is a good local ale."

The discussion at the bar had now turned to the forthcoming Champions League match. With Manchester City and Spurs still fighting their corner it could actually come back to England this year.

"Ben?" Alice said, obviously trying to recall his attention. "I said, can we drop by the hardware store on the way home? I want to pick up one of their brochures. It's about time we started looking at what's out there so that we can decide what we can do with our kitchen. I'd really like to be able to fit in a dishwasher."

Cooke realised that he hadn't heard her speak the first time, having been intent to listening to the conversation at the bar, so readily agreed, even though a kitchen refit wasn't top of his agenda for home improvements. He wasn't any good at DIY and so they would have to pay someone to do it.

Just as they were about to leave, his mobile phone started up its robust rendition of the 1812 overture.

"DCI Cooke." He listened for a while, then, "I'll be right there," he said.

"Sorry, love." He put the phone back in his pocket. "There have been some developments and I need to go in."

With a shrug of her shoulders, she announced, "I'll drop you back home so that you can take your own car, and I'll go back out to the retail park to pick up some brochures from B&Q. I'll find some flooring and paint samples as well while I'm there."

"The missing driver's only gone and turned up," he told her, as soon as they were out of earshot.

"Then we'd better not hang about, had we?" she said. Knowing he was keen to get into the office, within a few minutes she was driving out of the village and heading towards the main road.

SATURDAY 4TH MAY

Afternoon

Susan returned from the ice rink with Gina, having dropped off her friend Lucy on the way home. She was determined to try and keep things as normal as possible under the circumstances, and as both girls had been so looking forward to the outing, she had taken them. John was spending the day with his friend, Steve. They played football together for the local under 14s and Steve's father would take them to the match – the first ever that Tony would miss.

As she took off her coat, the phone began to ring, and she snatched it up. "Hello?"

"Sue, I'm so sorry, so sorry."

"Tony, where are you? Where have you been?" she screeched.

"I don't know, I've been walking all morning. I'm in some village." He sounded intensely weary.

There was a click and the line went dead.

Shocked and trembling, Susan sank to the floor, the receiver still in her hand.

On auto-pilot now, she dialled his mobile number, but it must have run out of power after all this time, she told herself, when there was no reply.

She looked up to find Gina staring at her.

"Was that Dad? Where is he? When's he coming home?"

"Yes, it was," she replied, , "He'll be home soon."

She had better let the police know that he was alive.

Not wanting her daughter to hear the next phone call, she floundered as she tried to think of somewhere to send her out of the way for a few minutes. She noticed an anniversary card addressed and stamped ready for posting next week, and she asked her daughter to pop to the post box with it.

As the front door closed behind her, Susan picked up the card the policewoman had left on the hall table and quickly dialled the number.

It was answered by the brusque voice of Sgt Brookes.

"This is Susan Hedges," she said. "My husband has just phoned me."

"Where is he?"

"He didn't know; he was cut off before I could ask him anything else. I tried to ring him back but there was no answer. His battery would be low after all this time."

"Did you dial 1471?"

"No, I assumed he must be on his mobile. I didn't think to, since he wouldn't have any charge. I'll do it now and ring you straight back."

She got a strange number when she tried, and wrote it down. She pressed 1 to return the call but it just rang out with no answer. Why hadn't she thought of that before?

She started to sob.

When would she see her soul mate again?

With a huge effort, she pulled herself together. She needed to let the police know the number so that he could be found and brought home.

DCI Cooke strode into the station and straight up to the counter.

The desk sergeant informed him that Tony Hedges had rung his wife at around midday. He had managed to tell her that he had been walking all morning and that he was in a phone box in a village somewhere, although he didn't know where, before he was cut off. She in turn had rung her local force to let them know he was alive.

Cooke dashed up to his office, dialled the number for the Gloucestershire police and asked to be put through to Sgt Brookes.

Once he had introduced himself, he asked about the phone call they had received. Brookes told him that they had traced the number to a small village south of Leeds. They had alerted the West Yorkshire police, who were now out looking for him.

Cooke told him that he wanted to speak to Hedges as soon as possible and could come down tomorrow.

"May I suggest that we have a word with him first, sir, as he's on our books reported as missing, and although Derbyshire area are thinking of him as a suspect for their crime, it will be better for us and Hedges' wife if we close our case and don't alert him to your suspicions at this juncture. I'll let you know once he's back home and we've finished with him. All being well, you can then come down on Monday, if that suits you?"

Cooke agreed to this. It wasn't the ideal way to spend a bank holiday, but he needed to interview the man as soon as he could. He gave Sgt Brookes his mobile number with instructions to phone him direct.

He called his DI to bring her up to date, but stressed that there was no need for her to come back in. She was spending the bank holiday in Sheffield, where she was visiting her parents and catching up with friends. There was no point ruining her weekend too. He would see her on Tuesday, bright and early.

While he was talking, Cooke noticed an envelope on the other side of his desk, next to his in-tray, and he reached for it. Forensics had sent through their report from the quarry site. There were photos of tyre prints from near the beginning of the track, where some areas had remained wet after last week's rain. There was also a clear footprint near the scene from what looked like a work boot with worn cleats, and measured to be a size 13. If that had anything to do with the case then that could be good news. Not many men had feet that big. They were looking at what sort of car fit the profile: a Mercedes or BMW possibly. At this point there was nothing to say it was part of this investigation, but it couldn't be discounted.

It was now a waiting game until he could talk to Tony Hedges; and with no idea of who the victim was, there wasn't much point in him wasting any more of his day off.

He closed the folder and decided to call it a day. Might as well enjoy what was left of the weekend. With any luck he could head down to Gloucestershire on Monday.

He rang to ask Alice if she wanted him to pick up a takeaway, and headed home a happy man when she told him she had bought a mezze of different meats and cheeses and some of his favourite walnut loaf.

SUNDAY 5TH MAY

Afternoon

Cooke and Alice were enjoying a lazy day at home. After their lovemaking in the warmth of the morning sun streaming through the bedroom window, he made them both coffee, and they spent the rest of the morning in bed happily reading the Sunday papers, every now and then commenting on something but otherwise in companionable silence.

Later, after a leisurely brunch of cold meats, cheeses, hummus and salad, leftovers from the night before, they looked through the kitchen brochures Alice had collected from B&Q and both agreed on modern cream-coloured units with a breakfast bar and wooden work surfaces.

"What colour paint do you think?" she asked as she passed him the colour chart.

"I don't know. You're far better at matching colours than me. I'd have magnolia everywhere."

"You would too," Alice said, rolling her eyes. "We need to go and have a look at the units anyway, to make sure they're okay. When will you be able to come with me?"

Cooke sighed, and Alice gave him a long-suffering look.

"I just can't make any promises, with this death to deal with. We still don't know who the poor chap is yet."

The telephone started to ring in the lounge.

Saved by the bell, Cooke thought as he went to answer it.

It was Sgt Ford. "Tony Hedges has been found and was brought home last night. They interviewed him this morning. He told them he'd been kept prisoner in some sort of agricultural building since Monday; and then on Saturday morning when he woke up, he found the door ajar. He is very anxious to help, and has shown them on a map where the delivery was made, but he's obviously reluctant to actually go back there."

"They were meant to ring me direct," Cooke complained. "I'll go down there tomorrow to speak to him."

"That's not necessary, sir, seeing as tomorrow's a bank holiday and Hedges wants to spend it with his family celebrating his daughter's birthday, which he missed. His boss has given him the rest of the week off to recover from his ordeal. Brookes said that as you have been good enough to let them close their case first, he'll have one of his men bring him here to Derbyshire on Tuesday morning. "

Although he wanted to speak to Hedges as soon as possible, Cooke accepted this plan; so unless anything else transpired, he would be able to take his wife for a much-needed day out to the seaside.

With this in mind, and to get Alice off his case, Cooke returned to the kitchen where she was stacking the plates next to the sink ready for washing, and asked, "What time does B&Q close today?"

Alice quickly looked it up on her phone and told him it was four o' clock on a Sunday.

"If we go straight away, we should be able to have a good look at the units before then," he said.

Alice hugged him, and went to take her car keys from the cast iron dog-shaped rack on the wall.

TUESDAY 7TH MAY

Morning

Craig was late getting to the office, and Trevor tapped his wristwatch as he saw him come in through the door, but didn't look to be too mad with him.

"Tony has turned up," he said as the younger man sat at his desk and logged in to his computer.

"That's great news. Where was he? Is he okay?"

"Boss says he was kidnapped at that Leeds drop and kept prisoner. Apparently, he has told the police where the delivery point was, so the local bobbies can go and check it out."

"Blimey!" Craig said, still thinking it was all his fault for taking on the booking.

"Graham has been out to see him and says he's happy to be back with his family, but obviously traumatised by his ordeal. He's been given the week off to get over it."

"What a dreadful thing to happen. Do the others know?"

"Yes, Graham was here when I got here this morning and told everyone as they came in."

Jenny arrived. "Hello, boys!" she called as she headed for her office.

"Have a good time?" Craig asked.

"Yes, it was very pleasant. Mum was really well, and we had a lovely walk along the old train line footpath to Chesil Beach yesterday before I headed home."

"Graham wants to see you," Trevor told her.

She looked worried. 'What's that about, then?'

"A lot has happened since you were here last Tuesday and he wants to tell you before you hear it from someone else."

Jenny took off her coat, then headed straight towards the boss's office and knocked at the door.

Cooke left his car in its allotted space and was in a good mood as he walked past the horse chestnut tree in the market square. The pink candles were flowering on its branches and a grey squirrel darted up the trunk at his approach, but was soon lost in the lush foliage. He and Alice had spent a rare day out in Skegness yesterday, and the bank holiday traffic had not been too bad, probably due to the fact that there was a rather sneaky cold breeze and people had decided to stay at home.

The lorry driver was supposed to be coming to see him, so he needed to find out if there was any news yet on the victim's identity.

His sergeant had nothing new to report so he made his way up to his office, where Sharon was already waiting for him.

"Did you have a good weekend?" he asked.

"Yes, it was awesome. Managed to catch up with a lot of old mates."

"Anything to report?"

"Jimmy has managed to find the former owners of the quarry, and they will send a list of personnel who worked there in the last three years of trading." She consulted her notes. "They purchased the quarry from a Barry Wright, the heir of the previous owner, who didn't want to take over the business, so they don't have any information from before that date. Nothing yet from the social media aspect or the press release on who the tattoo belonged to."

"I have Tony Hedges coming to see me this morning. It seems he is anxious to help us with our enquiries."

"Wow! That's a turn up."

They were interrupted as the front desk rang through to say their visitor had arrived. Cooke asked that he been shown into the interview room.

He invited Sharon to come with him.

"Mr Hedges, I'm DCI Cooke and this is DI Williams. Thank you for coming to see us."

"No problem," replied Tony. "I just want to help."

"Would you like a drink? Tea, coffee?"

"Yes, please. Tea, milk, two sugars"

Sharon left to ask one of the clerical staff to bring the drink with a couple of biscuits.

As this was not an official interview, Cooke didn't turn on the tape, but he informed their guest that Sharon would take notes. Gloucestershire already had a signed statement from the man.

On Sharon's return she took her seat next to her boss and opposite the driver, and Cooke began to run through his questions.

"You collected from Cotswold Chemicals on Monday morning?"

"Yes, it was an extra job that Craig had added at the last minute. "

"Was it a smooth collection?"

"No. I had a job to find them, and had to ask the young girl at Juicy Fruits. She thought there was someone new at the unit at the far end."

"What was the customer like?"

"Scruffy hair, boiler suit, about my age, I guess – early forties."

"And he gave you the address the goods had to go to, and paid you?"

"Yes. He had to go and write out a delivery note. It wasn't on headed paper, and he said that his stationery hadn't arrived yet."

"Would it surprise you to learn that there is no company of that name at the Bullnose Farm business centre?"

Tony looked puzzled. "Well, yes, since I picked up a load there."

Cooke produced a map of the Leeds area. "Can you show me where the delivery was made?"

Hedges studied it and pointed. "It was there."

"What can you tell me about the place, the people?"

"The premises was called Ash Farm and seemed deserted and pretty derelict, but there was someone inside. I rang the bell and he shouted that he would open the doors, so I went to drop down the tail lift to take the goods off."

"What did he look like?" asked Sharon.

"I didn't see him. I was at the back of the wagon and had my back to the barn. The doors were open when I looked again. There was no sign of him, so I guess he was behind the open door."

"Did he have an accent?"

"Yeah, he was definitely from round that way."

"What happened then?" Cooke asked.

"That's the last I can remember. I was at the back of the wagon letting down the tail lift. The next thing I knew I was lying on the floor of a barn. I tried the door but it wouldn't open. I was locked in, and there was a big bar across the outside. My watch was missing and so was my mobile phone."

"What about the windows?"

"There was only one small window, high up above the door."

"Could you see anything in the room?"

"There was a box with packets of crisps in it and a case of diet coke by the door – oh, and an empty plastic bucket in the corner."

"It sounds like whoever left you there didn't want you to starve," Cooke said.

Hedges shrugged. "Crisps aren't any substitute for proper food. I was so hungry."

"Did you try to escape?"

"Of course I did! I was desperate to break out of there. I had no idea where I was, or if there were people close by. I shouted and made as much noise as I could, but no-one came. The whole time I was there I didn't hear a single vehicle come near the place. The window was too high to get to, and no matter how hard I kicked and hit the door, it wouldn't budge." His hands grasped each other until the knuckles were white. "I was imprisoned, no one was coming to help me. I thought I'd never get to see or speak to my family again. I missed my daughter's birthday, for God's sake! Of course I tried to escape!"

His voice broke, and he wiped at his eyes. "Sorry," he said.

Cooke waited for him to compose himself.

"How did you get out?" he asked softly.

"I found the door open a crack when I woke."

"That was Saturday morning?"

"I didn't know that then. I'd lost all sense of time, but it was light outside."

Cooke's instinct told him that this man was telling the truth, so they had no real reason to hold him. It wouldn't hurt to keep him on the back burner though.

"Thank you again for coming," Cooke said, bringing the interview to a close. "I just need to get your fingerprints taken to eliminate them from any we may find at the site. If you remember anything else, please give me a call." He took a card from his inside jacket pocket and handed it over.

He got up, and Sharon ushered Hedges out of the room while Cooke dashed up to his office to ring the scene of crime guys. He needed them to go and look at this derelict building on the edge of Leeds, as a matter of urgency.

WEDNESDAY 8TH MAY

Morning

As Cooke walked into the main office, he looked around at his team to make sure no one was on the phone before he started to speak.

"Can I have every one's attention please," he said, raising his voice above the general hubbub of conversation.

Everyone stopped talking.

"This will be brief." He walked to the far corner of the room. "Tony Hedges came to see me yesterday of his own accord to tell us his version of the events of Monday last. He says he was taken prisoner at the delivery point, which he was able to indicate on a map, and only escaped on Saturday morning when he found that the previously barred door had been left open. Scene of crime went to the site yesterday afternoon and found evidence that someone had been staying in the barn on the abandoned farm near Leeds which seems to confirm his story – crisp packets, empty coke cans and a full bucket in the corner. They are going back today to continue their search."

"Could he have planted evidence himself for us to find?" asked DS Golding.

"It's possible, but to be honest my gut feeling is that he is telling the truth. He did come up to see us voluntarily; but we will still keep him in mind for the time being."

Looking around at his team, Cooke continued, "We still have no idea who was killed, or even if they were unlawfully killed, and why. Anyone got anything to report?"

"We had a couple of hits on Facebook," Jimmy replied, " but after following them up it transpired that they were both alive and well and their tattoos were not all that similar."

"It's in the local paper?"

"Yes."

"Any results?"

"Nothing yet, just morons wasting our time."

"Perhaps we need to cast our net a bit further afield. Get it in the local press for the Leeds area, Jimmy."

"What about Gloucestershire? He still might be someone that Hedges knows."

"I don't think so; we'll just leave it at Leeds for now."

He walked over to the white board.

"What we really need is a name for this man," he continued, prodding at the tattoo photo with his finger. "Until we know that, we can't hope to find a motive. Someone must be missing him."

"Why pick a site in Gloucestershire for the collection?" asked Golding.

"It could be because whoever it was knew the haulier delivered in Yorkshire every week. Possibly someone from one of the companies that they delivered to or from. It was a regular run," suggested Sharon.

"That's a good point," Cooke said. "Get a list of companies they have delivered to in the area since, say, the beginning of the year, and where they collected from, then follow them up."

"It puts our Mr Hedges back in the frame," the DS pointed out.

"That's true. We need to check CCTV between Leeds and Wellsend to try and discover what route the vehicle took."

"I'll get onto that."

"Any questions? " Cooke looked round the room.

No-one spoke. "OK. I'm heading out to Leeds to have a look myself, and find out what more the guys have found. Keep me informed of any developments."

THURSDAY 9TH MAY

Morning

"Good morning, sir," the desk sergeant said, as Cooke approached his counter. "I have just taken an interesting call."

"Really?"

"It was a woman from Huddersfield," he went on, reading from a piece of paper as he picked it up from the desk. "Name of Elizabeth Clarke. Says she thought she recognised the tattoo, or at least the design. It matched one she had in front of her, on an invoice from a couple of years ago."

Cooke thanked him, then took the stairs two at a time and dialled the Huddersfield number as soon as he reached his desk. He introduced himself and went on to ask her about the design.

Sharon walked in to find Cooke on the phone, and stopped dead in her tracks as she realised her boss was on to something.

She stood listening as he finished the call and waited for him to speak.

Pointing at the phone, he told her, "That might be a really good lead. A woman from Huddersfield who seems pretty convinced that she has an invoice in her possession from a graphic design outfit in Leeds with a logo very similar to that tattoo."

"That's great. It might be the break we've been waiting for," enthused his assistant. "Why has it taken her so long to come forward?"

"Apparently she's spent the past two weeks travelling round Italy with her husband. They had decided to have a complete break from the internet, so took their cameras and left their phones at home. She's only just catching up. Anyway, she saw our appeal and went to look out the invoice which, in her opinion, matches the tattoo."

"Did I hear you say you would go up there to see her?"

"Yes, she gave me the address from the invoice, but doesn't think they are there any more. Her husband is a plumber and used the same person to design his logo for him, as it was a mate of his from school, so he may have more information for us."

"Do you want me to come along?"

"No, I'll leave you in charge here. Have you got that list from the haulage firm yet?"

"Yes, they faxed it over last night."

"Follow that up; find out if any of the warehouse staff were absent on the fateful Monday at the end of April."

"Will do, guv."

"I'll catch up with Dave Akers while I'm in the Leeds area, as it might be helpful to get him on board. I can't help but think that the answers all lie in Yorkshire."

Dave had been his DI not so long ago but had taken a promotion that had come up in Leeds. Sharon was very good at her job, but he did miss the male camaraderie he'd enjoyed with her predecessor.

"Anything else you would like me to do in your absence?"

"Have a brainstorming session with the team. We need to find out more about the Cotswold Chemicals guy. He told the driver that he had only just moved in. Has he been trading elsewhere under a different name? He must have rented the unit in Longburrow - who did he rent it from and how did he pay?"

He picked up the slip of paper on which he had been writing, saying, "If this lead is any good then we should soon have a name for that poor sod at the quarry."

With that he picked up his car keys and headed for the door.

He went home and packed an overnight bag, just in case, and left a note for Alice to let her know where he had gone, saying he would ring her later.

THURSDAY 9TH MAY

Afternoon

It was nudging midday by the time he approached Huddersfield, so he stopped and bought a sandwich from a garage to eat after he'd been to see Mr Clarke.

With the aid of his Satnav he was soon able to locate the row of soot-grimed, back-to-back terraced houses where the Clarkes lived, and found their home up a dirt track to the back of the main row. He was greeted at the door by an auburn-haired woman in her mid-thirties.

"Peter won't be long," she said. "He's been called out to attend to a small leak. Take a seat. "

The front door opened straight into a living room, where a sofa and an armchair faced the corner niche which housed a TV. There were shelves of trophies, which upon closer inspection revealed themselves to be for football.

Cooke sat down on the sofa and Mrs Clarke picked up the invoice from the windowsill.

As she handed it over the door opened and in strode Peter Clarke, wearing navy work trousers and a less than white tee-shirt, a mass of mousey shoulder-length hair tied back with a piece of string. He told Cooke that Liz had texted him to tell him that he had arrived, and asked how he could help.

"She said that it had something to do with Dick Fox, who did my logo for me," he said.

"Yes, we are trying to identify the victim of an accident, and your wife says that the logo on his invoice is very similar to the rather distinctive tattoo on the man's arm. I have to say it does look very much like it."

Hearing this, Peter sank into the nearby armchair.

Cooke noted the reaction. "Could you tell me more about your friend, such as where the business moved to?"

"Oh lord, I hope it isn't him! We were good mates at school," Peter said. "He set up the business with his girlfriend, Carole, after meeting her at University here in Huddersfield. She was a year younger than him but he took a gap year before starting the course. They called it Black Fox Design - an amalgamation of their two names - and he was proud of the logo which they had worked on together. They made a wonderful job of mine too. I was really pleased with it."

He walked across the room to a small set of drawers and handed over a piece of headed paper featuring a cartoon plumber, spanner in hand, with Peter Clarke, Plumbing and Heating in gothic print. He sat down heavily again.

"Your wife tells me that he's moved."

"Yes, it was really sad. Carole was pregnant with their first child and was suffering from horrendous morning sickness, so he left her in bed one morning and went into the office alone. They say that he must have left the mobile gas heater on and as he closed the front door, the draught blew the curtain into the flame. The whole place went up – she didn't stand a chance."

Tears filled his eyes as he looked up at Cooke.

"After the inquest he shut up shop and vanished. I don't know where he went to. Oh, I really hope it isn't him!"

"Does he still have family living in Leeds?"

"He was an only child, and lived with his mother. His father died when he was young."

He scribbled something on a piece of paper. "This is where they lived in Harehills when we were at school; his mother's probably still there."

Cooke thanked him for his help and left.

He climbed back into his car and unwrapped the rather soggy sandwich, took a bite, set it down on its plastic bag, and dialled up Dave Akers' number.

"Hello, old buddy, I'm in your neck of the woods, and wondered if you fancied meeting up for a pint?"

After arranging the time and place, Cooke booked himself into the Novotel in the city centre, finished his lunch, and set off to the address that he had been given by Peter Clarke.

He drew up, studying the nice little house with its neat garden. Net curtains festooned the windows, obscuring the inside from view. He knocked at the pillar-box red door.

"She'll be down the old folks' home," a voice called from behind him.

"I'm looking for a Mrs Fox. Does she live here?" Cooke enquired of the elderly man who stood on the pavement.

"Yes, Brenda lives here, but she'll be running the bingo at the old folks' home this afternoon."

"Oh, thanks. Do you know what time she'll be back?"

"I think she goes on from there to her office cleaning job. She's usually in most mornings."

Cooke decided he would call back tomorrow. It would soon be time to catch up with his old mate, so he set the Satnav and pointed his car in the direction of the public house which Dave had suggested. He was a bit early so pulled up in the car park, phoned Alice, and set off for a wander down the street to kill time.

He did a bit of window shopping before coming to a second-hand book shop. Never able to pass such an establishment without having a look inside, he found a Peter Robinson novel which he hadn't read. He paid for it and strolled back to the pub, dropping the book into his car before going inside.

He soon found Dave, sitting at a small round table in the corner of the rather dark lounge with two pints in front of him.

"The guest beer this week is Copper Dragon and I can highly recommend it," he said as he gestured towards his friend's glass.

"Cheers!" Cooke took a swig of the dark honey brown beer.

"What brings you up to the big city?" Dave enquired as he passed the menu to his pal.

Cooke explained about the death on his patch and how a lead had brought him up to Dave's neck of the woods.

"Could you find out anything you've got on a fire that happened about two years ago? It was in the Horsforth district. A young pregnant woman, Carole Black, sadly died. It's her boyfriend, Richard Fox, who we believe may be the victim of our explosion. From what I'm told her death was a tragic accident, but that is only hearsay, so I'd like to find out more about it."

"No probs, mate."

"I'll pay for the food," Cooke told him as he looked at the menu and decided on the lamb hotpot. Dave chose the fish and chips, and Cooke went to order and pay.

While they waited for their meals to arrive, Cooke filled his friend in on the changes at his old workplace, and learnt that Dave and his wife had settled well into their new home and jobs.

As they ate, he went on to tell his pal more about the explosion and how it certainly seemed like foul play. He said he intended to speak to the possible victim's mother in the morning before heading back to Derbyshire. They parted company in the car park and Dave promised he would look into the fire to see if there was anything suspicious there.

Cooke returned to his hotel and ordered a brandy nightcap before turning in for the night with his new book.

FRIDAY 10TH MAY

Morning

"I don't know whether to give Tony his usual run for Monday," Trevor told his boss. "Leo did it this week and got on all right."

"I think we should try and keep things as normal as we can for him. It will be odd enough that he has to drive a strange wagon, even though it's a newer model," Graham replied. "Have you got the livery booked?"

"Yes, but they can't do it until next weekend."

"We'll have to live with that then."

"At least all the trackers were put in last weekend, and they are doing Tony's today."

Trevor went back to his desk and started booking the load onto the computer.

"Chelsea are in the final," Craig greeted him as he arrived for work.

"You'll be pleased about that," replied Trevor with little enthusiasm. Unlike most of his colleagues he wasn't a big football fan.

"Yes, if they win, it means that they're guaranteed a place in the Champions League next year."

"That's good." There was a short pause. "Tony will be back on Monday and doing his normal run."

This brought Craig back down to earth with a bang. He wasn't really looking forward to seeing Tony after all that had happened.

Realising this, Trevor offered to do the early shift on Monday, and Craig readily accepted.

After a full English breakfast, Cooke paid his tab, making sure to collect a receipt for expenses, and headed back to Harehills to speak to Mrs Fox.

This time the door was opened by a woman dressed in a floral tee-shirt and black slacks, who he guessed to be in her late fifties.

"Mrs Fox?"

"Yes. Who wants to know?"

"DCI Cooke from Derbyshire Police." He showed his ID. "May I come in?"

"What could you possibly want with me?" she demanded, standing her ground.

"It's about your son, Richard."

"He can't be in any trouble. He's a good boy. What's happened to him?"

"Can I come in, please? This would be much better discussed indoors."

With some reluctance she stood back and allowed him to enter, and led the way into a tidy, well-appointed living room. Delicate leaves wound their way around the walls on the tasteful wallpaper and the furniture gleamed brightly in the morning sunshine. She sat in what was obviously her favourite armchair and gestured for him to sit on the green faux leather sofa.

"What's this all about then?" she asked, looking worried.

"There has been an explosion in a quarry near Matlock," Cooke said, "and we are trying to establish the identity of someone involved. The only thing we have to work on is a tattoo. Does your son have any tattoos?"

"Yes, he has the Leeds badge on his leg. Had it done as soon as he was old enough. Always been a Leeds supporter."

"Did he have any others – a dog, maybe?"

"Oh yes – well, it's a black fox on his arm. He designed it with Carole and they both had one done at the same time. She was his partner - they didn't believe in marriage. They had the tattoos done as a sort of bond."

"I have a photo of the tattoo in question and a friend of his says it is very like the design that Richard had on his invoices." He pulled the photo out of the envelope he was carrying and handed it to her.

"Mrs Fox, do you confirm that this is your son's tattoo?" She nodded. "I'm sorry, but it does look as though it was your son who was killed in the explosion."

"Oh, my God!" she cried, as tears sprang to her eyes. "Oh dear, oh dear, oh dear. Oh, my darling Ricky!"

Cooke handed her a tissue from the box on the nearby coffee table.

"What was he doing in the quarry? He can't have been working there. He told me he'd got a job in a warehouse. I said it was a waste, with his talents."

"We don't know, I'm afraid; we are still trying to piece it all together, but we think he may have been the passenger in a lorry which had an accident."

Mrs Fox just looked dazed.

"Could you let me have his address?"

"Yes, you'll probably find him there, right as rain."

Cooke thought not. "I hope so," he said.

"He told me not to tell anyone his whereabouts, I don't know why, but I guess that wouldn't include the police," she said as she handed him a small piece of paper from her address book.

"Have you told anyone where he is living?"

"Only Nancy, who's been my friend forever. He wouldn't mind me telling her."

"Is there anyone I can ring to come and be with you?"

"Nancy, she lives two doors down. I'll go and see her."

Cooke waited while she locked up and walked with her to her friend's house. He explained to Nancy that her neighbour had had a nasty shock, and as he did so, Mrs Fox broke down in tears and fell into her friend's arms.

"I'll look after her," Nancy said.

"We'll be in touch as soon as we know any more, Mrs Fox," was Cooke's parting remark as he watched her being led inside.

Back at his car, he phoned Sharon with the name and address of the possible victim.

"I need a couple of men to go over to Wellsend and firstly see if Richard Fox is at home, which is very doubtful, as I'm pretty sure it was him, and if not, to go house to house in his street to find out if anyone has seen him, or noticed anything unusual. I want the reports on my desk by tomorrow morning."

Knowing that his partner would move quickly, Cooke soon left Leeds behind and was sailing down the M1 in the direction of home.

He was just about to leave the motorway and take the country route when his hands-free started to ring, cutting out the news report. It was Sharon, reporting that there was no one at home at the house. PC Milner went round the back and discovered a broken window in the door, the glass left where it had fallen. A neighbour popped her head over the fence to find out what was going on and, when asked, said she hadn't seen Richard for a few days.

She thought he must have gone on holiday somewhere. The boys would start the house to house right away, and Sharon had sent the scene of crime guys over.

SATURDAY 11TH MAY

Morning

Cooke logged into his computer and scrolled through his emails. He found one from Dave Akers with attachments so printed it all off to read through later.

He had come in to find out what yesterday's house to house had turned up. PC Milner had stayed late to type up his report as promised and it was sitting on his desk. The neighbour who they had spoken to had been away on holiday last week and had only got back this Monday night. There were quite a few people not at home, and while it was doubtful, if they worked, that they would have been in on the day in question, he and his partner would go out again this morning in hope of finding someone in.

A lot of folk had seen the lorry parked in the street and had wondered what it was doing there; most guessed that it must have broken down. An elderly lady, Mrs Celia Fletcher, who had been sitting in her favourite armchair by the window, watching the world go by, said that she had seen the lorry pull up, and noted that it was still there at bedtime. She didn't know when it had left, and was a bit vague about who had been driving the vehicle. Although she had seen him, she hadn't actually got a look at his face; but he was quite well built and had dark, curly hair. He had been wearing denim jeans and a green shirt. He had gone to the back of the house through a side gate.

Mr Lionel Shaw had been passing by the parked lorry at about nine, on his way home from the pub, when he literally bumped into a man who he had assumed to be the driver, wheeling a box-type pallet backwards from the house to the vehicle. He said the man was stocky with short, dark curly hair and dark, probably brown eyes. He hadn't noticed anyone else. He would come in on Monday to work on a photo-fit.

Cooke crossed to the printer and picked up the email from Dave, which was just a cover note for the attached newspaper report. He quickly scanned through the email. The coroner at the inquest had recorded the death of Richard Fox's partner as accidental. He was about to look at the attachment when, glancing at the date on his desk calendar, he realised it was his wedding anniversary. He slid the email and newspaper report into the file and headed for Tesco, which was on the way home and would be able to provide him with the necessary card, flowers and chocolates. He would have to see if he could book a table at the new authentic Italian in town too.

MONDAY 13TH MAY

Morning

Tony was feeling a bit apprehensive about his return to work this morning. Although it was back to the usual routine, it would never be quite the same again. He had spent a wonderful week with his family as it was half term, and they had worked hard to try and bring some normality back into the children's lives.

He looked at the school photos on the mantelpiece as he walked to the door. Susan followed, kissed him goodbye and watched as he drove off.

When he walked through the office door there was a big cheer from Trevor and a couple of the drivers, Leo and Andy, who were collecting the day's details.

"All right, mate?" Andy said as he left clutching his load sheet.

Tony felt strange and somewhat overwhelmed. "Yes, thanks," was all he could manage.

Leo gave him a hug. "It's good to see you back."

He had a sudden flash of a memory, but it left just as quickly as it had come. He shook his head and tried to concentrate on what Leo was saying to him.

Trevor nipped back to his desk to get the air freshener, leaving Tony telling Leo he would be in touch later.

After a quick spray, Trevor asked him how he was feeling

"I'm not really sure. I'm okay, course I am. I'll be all right once I'm back behind the wheel."

"I did think about giving you a different run, but Graham said it would probably be better to keep it normal. A bit like 'hair of the dog', I guess," he smiled. "You'll be driving the new eighteen tonner, but it's not liveried up yet. They're coming to do that at the weekend."

"I'll miss old Betsie, but I'm sure I'll soon get used to the new truck."

"Well, here are your notes. Just the normal run to Sheffield then a drop in Halifax before ending up at Carlisle for the usual pickup."

"Thanks, Trev." Tony took his papers and headed to his car, took out his new sleeping bag and overnight bag and plodded off towards the shiny new green truck.

MONDAY 13TH MAY

Evening

Arthur was a miserable old sod. He always had something to moan about, and at sixty-eight he thought he had a good right to speak up.

He had moved to the Cotswolds three years ago, when he retired from the rat race in London, believing the country air would be good for his asthma.

His wife, Betty, three years his junior, had taken to the new life like a duck to water, and was very soon involved with the local bowls club and had even joined the small town's rambling group.

He, on the other hand, didn't like the noise of the birds, the countryside smells, the way horses ambled along the narrow country lanes, or the strange eerie noises of the night. The one thing he did like was the local pub, which he would visit each evening, and where he would moan about the ills of the day to anyone who would listen.

For a couple of weeks now he had been grumbling about a van which had been parked outside his house. It had appeared one day and hadn't moved since. He'd asked all the neighbours if it was theirs or someone visiting them, and was no nearer to finding the owner, to whom he would give a good piece of his mind when he did eventually find them.

"Oh no, here he comes," muttered the barman to his young barmaid, as he saw Arthur coming through the door.

Arthur closed in on the bar as someone yelled, "Car gone yet?"

"It's not a car; it's a bloody van of some sort," snarled Arthur. "Been there two weeks now and getting dirtier by the day – covered in bird shit. A bloody eyesore!"

"Perhaps you should contact the police. They'll be able to find out who it belongs to and ask them to move it," suggested the barmaid.

"I'll do that," Arthur announced. "I'll drive over to town tomorrow and see them."

"Don't forget to write down the number plate, as I'll doubt they'll bother to come out and look at it."

"No, they're far too busy harassing poor drivers," replied Arthur, who still hadn't forgotten the speeding fine he had been given ten years ago.

With that he settled down in the inglenook by the empty grate and started to complain to a couple of local workmen, who had been enjoying a quiet pint before heading home, about the cat which had sprayed up his front door last night, the smell of which had invaded the whole house.

TUESDAY 14TH MAY

Morning

It was a horrible drive along the Fosse Way and Arthur had to brake hard a couple of times, once for a pesky pheasant; he would have hit it but Betty screamed for him not to. The second time was because some bloody idiot was overtaking on a blind bend. The streets of London were never like this – so much safer!

He dropped Betty off outside the abbey in the town centre so she could have a look round the shops, and went to look for the police station. He found it quite easily and was able to park in their car park, although whether he was meant to was another question.

He locked up and marched up the steps to the big wooden door.

There was a uniformed officer manning the desk and talking on the phone. Arthur waited impatiently for him to finish.

"Yes, sir," the officer said as he hung up.

"I've come to report a van which has been sat outside my house for at least two weeks and not budged in that time. It's now covered in bird shit and looks like it's been abandoned, and I want it moved."

"Very well, sir, if you would like to wait over there," he pointed towards a hard wooden bench against the wall, "I'll find someone to come and take some details from you."

Arthur went and sat down, muttering to himself.

After about five minutes a smartly dressed young woman introduced herself as PCSO Davies and ushered him to a little room along the corridor. It was painted in institutional green and had a small window through which he could just see the branches of a tree outside.

"Now then, sir, may I take your name?" she asked.

"Arthur Chandler."

"And your address?"

"65 The Larches, Moretown."

"Is this where the vehicle is situated?"

"Yes, and it's a bloody eyesore."

"Can you give me the vehicle's details? What make of van is it?" she calmly continued.

"Mitsubishi."

"And what colour?"

"White – or at least it was."

"Do you have the registration number?"

Arthur looked out the scrap of paper and plonked it down on the desk.

"Thank you, sir. That's very helpful."

Making a note of the number, she told him that she would log it onto the computer and they should be able to find the owner and contact them. She pointed out that if the vehicle was taxed and it hadn't been stolen, there was nothing they could do as it was legally parked.

She accompanied him to the door and bade him goodbye.

Arthur walked back to his car. He knew he shouldn't have parked under that tree. The birds had already used the roof for target practice. He took a tissue from his pocket and wiped off the offending deposit. He'd drive round and find a space in one of the backstreets - no point in wasting money in the council car park. He should have time to look in the bookies before meeting Betty at the cafe as arranged.

Clutching his betting slips, Arthur left Corals and headed to the marketplace where the bakery housed a small cafe. Betty waved at him from her seat on the far side of the room.

"I've ordered a pot of tea and one of their amazing lardy cakes," she told him as he sat down.

She was eager to show him her bargains, and he told her that he wasn't very hopeful of the vehicle being moved in the near future.

"They said they would log it onto the computer," he told her, as though convinced that was the last they'd hear of it, and bit into the warm, calorie-laden cake.

"I doubt if the owner will be pleased that it's been found if they dumped it there because it had run out of tax."

"Time will tell I suppose. At least I have done my civic duty, and I'll be glad to see the back of it."

They drove home in silence, broken every now and then by Arthur's expletives at the inadequacies of other drivers.

They glided into the Larches and didn't initially notice the space where the van had been standing.

"It's gone!" exclaimed Arthur as he got out to have a good stretch.

"So it has."

"Trust the owner to come and move it on the very day I report it being there," he muttered.

"Well, it's certainly good to see the back of it," replied his wife.

TUESDAY 14TH MAY

Afternoon

"Jarvis Chemicals," Frank answered his phone rather abruptly, as he had been working on a price schedule for the restaurant chain for which he had just secured the first orders.

Jane came back into the office and heard him confirm that he was Frank Jarvis, the proprietor of the business, and was intrigued to find out what the conversation, which she only had one half of, was about.

"Well, I'm buggered!" Frank announced as he put the receiver back down. "That was Bedford police. Our pickup has turned up in Gloucestershire, of all places, minus the goods, of course."

"When can we go and fetch it?"

"Well, not for a couple of days. They have to do forensic tests as they think the chemical it was carrying may have been used in a crime. They need to go over it with a fine-toothed comb before they will let us have it back."

Jane looked worried. "I do hope Michael isn't involved in whatever it is. The stag weekend was at a hotel in Tewkesbury, and that's in Gloucestershire."

"Well, I was also told that a high-ranking man from Derbyshire police," he looked at the name he had scribbled down, "a DCI Cooke, would be getting in touch, which is really strange if the wagon turned up in Gloucestershire."

It was late that afternoon when DCI Cooke rang and arranged to come down and see them the following morning.

Given the man's senior rank, and although their son had adamantly stuck to his story that he had locked the pickup and the compound and put the keys back into the office, Frank and Jane were beginning to worry again that he might have been involved in its disappearance after all.

WEDNESDAY 15TH MAY

Morning

DCI Cooke made an early start for his journey to see Frank Jarvis. From what he had understood from the local force the pickup and its payload had been reported missing back in April, and they were of the opinion that it was an inside job. The son had nicked it himself or made it easy for whoever did. Either way, he was the only one they had in the frame, although they had no evidence.

Frank heard the vehicle pull up outside the office and was waiting for Cooke in the doorway.

"Frank Jarvis?" Cooke asked as he approached, his ID in his hand.

"Yes, come on in."

Cooke smelt the aroma of freshly brewed coffee and was pleased to be offered a cup as Frank showed him to an empty desk.

"I must say, I'm rather confused to be receiving a visit from Derbyshire if the truck was found in Gloucestershire," he said, as he placed a large mug in front of the police officer.

"It's a tenuous link," Cooke told him, "but the sort of chemical that went missing with your vehicle was used in a crime we are investigating in our area."

Frank went noticeably paler as he sat down.

"I believe your son was the last person to see the truck before it vanished?"

"Well, yes, he insists it was locked up in the compound on the Friday afternoon and the keys had been brought back in here."

"Who else was working here that day?"

"Me; the missus was here in the morning too. I have a little Ford Courier which Tim, one of my drivers, was using for a few deliveries in Cambridge. Joe, the warehouseman, was off on holiday, so Michael, my son, was helping get the orders ready for the following week."

"Is that all?"

"Yes, we are really a small concern. I'm trying to specialise in cleaning products, but we also have the peroxide which I have been selling to hair salons."

"So you haven't been in the business long then? What did you do before?"

"I was a rep for a chemical firm up north. When Jane's father had a stroke, she wanted to move down this way to be nearer her parents. We had a bit of savings and I decided to launch out on my own, using my contacts from up there."

"Whereabouts up north?"

"Tyneside, although I am originally from the home counties."

That explained the lack of a northern accent.

"I could do with names and addresses for everyone working here at the time."

"I'll get Jane to find them out for you – she'll be here soon."

"I'd also like to see your son too, while I'm here. Where can I find him?"

"He's at work."

"And where is that?"

"It won't look good, having the police turn up to see him there," Frank hesitated.

"I need to speak to him before I head back home."

Frank reluctantly wrote down the name and address and handed it over.

Jane came in at that moment, and Frank filled her in on the conversation so far and asked her to dig out the names and addresses of their employees.

She soon found the relevant files, photocopied them and put them into an A4 envelope with a compliments slip, before handing them over.

"Thank you. Now if you'll excuse me, I must go and see your son."

"Wait a minute," Jane hurried after him. "I forgot, we had Techie here then setting up the web site. I'll just go and find his invoice, as it will have his address."

A few moments later she returned, frowning down at a piece of paper. "I'm afraid there isn't an address," she apologised, as she handed it over. "We paid him by bank transfer so his bank details are there along with his name."

Cooke glanced at it. "Where was he from, do you know?"

"I don't," Frank admitted. "He advertises on Facebook. I liked the look of his work, and he's not too expensive either. He uses a mobile number and I hadn't thought to ask him. He said he could come down in his little VW camper van and live in that while he was doing the work. Parked it round the corner on the waste land there." As an afterthought he said, "From his accent, I would say he was originally from Yorkshire."

Cooke thanked them both, and closed the door behind

him.

He used his mobile to look up the postcode for the company where Michael Jarvis worked, and punched it into the Sat Nav. It didn't take long to find the place.

"Good morning, how can I help you?" enquired the middle-aged receptionist.

"DCI Cooke from Derbyshire police," he said, showing his ID. "I would like to have a word with one of your employees, please."

"I'll fetch the manager for you," she stated and went through to the office.

She soon came back with a smartly dressed young man, who introduced himself as Sam Mason.

"Who is it you want to speak to?" he asked.

"Michael Jarvis."

"Should I be worried? Has he done anything wrong?"

"Not as far as I'm aware. I just need his help in an investigation, that's all."

"I'll go and find him for you. You can use my dad's office." He gestured to Cooke to precede him to a spacious room divided off from one corner of the main space.

"Take a seat," he said. "I'll be just a minute."

Cooke sat and looked around him while he waited. The desk was a beautiful antique mahogany and carried a large black leather desk pad, with a matching desk diary set to its right and an expensive-looking pen holder which appeared to be made of ebony and silver. A standard black telephone sat to the left. Impressive, he thought, with just a touch of jealousy.

The door opened and in walked a rather timid-looking lad with a striking resemblance to Frank Jarvis.

"You wanted to speak to me?"

"Yes, sit down, lad." Cooke pointed to the chair opposite

his own. "It's about the theft of your father's pick up. The matter has now become rather more serious."

The boy looked terrified

"Are you sure that you locked the vehicle away in the compound on the evening of Friday, 26th April, after loading it with the pallet of peroxide?"

"I'm certain I did it. Absolutely positive."

"I hear you went on a stag weekend afterwards?"

"Yes, in Tewkesbury. My best mate is getting married next month. We had a great weekend, played golf, although I'm useless, and went paint-balling. That was more my idea of fun."

"How did you get to Tewkesbury?"

"I went by rail. I caught the train just after 5pm. I had wanted to catch an earlier one so there was only one change, but I had to work for Dad."

Cooke thought this might have made the lad careless with locking up and made a note of it.

"Did you travel alone?"

"Yes - everyone else was coming from elsewhere."

"How did you get to the station?"

"Dad paid for a cab because I was running late, and he had already had a drink when he arrived home."

"What taxi firm was it?"

Michael told him and Cooke rose to leave.

"I won't keep you from your work any longer, though I may wish to speak to you again."

When he reached his car Cooke phoned through to Sharon and asked her to put the names he had been given by Frank Jarvis into the computer to see what it turned up.

THURSDAY 16TH MAY

Morning

Cooke arrived at his desk to find several sheets of paper had been left for him, so he settled down to read through them. They were mostly day to day trivia such as expenses sheets and local crime reports, but there was also a list of the personnel who had worked at the quarry while the last owners were there. He glanced at it, and put it in the file.

He opened his computer and found an e-mail from Gloucestershire saying that they had found a bandana under the front seat of the pickup truck and had extracted some good hair samples from it. They had attached a colour photo of a yellow bandana with a black and white yin-yang design. He would email this to Frank Jarvis to see if he recognised it as belonging to anyone on his staff.

At that moment Sharon came in with coffee for the two of them and confirmed that she had entered the list onto the computer along with all the names from Jarvis Chemicals.

Cooke remembered the possible lead and told Sharon about it as he forwarded the photo of the bandana to Jarvis, along with a covering note.

"With our luck it will belong to the regular driver," he said, as he pressed 'Send'.

"Do you want anything from Lettuce Eat today?" she asked as she handed him the menu. This deli was proving to be very popular amongst the staff as it offered some excellent baguettes and changed the fillings on the menu daily.

"I'll have a look and take it down to Sara," he said, his mind elsewhere.

As luck would have it, Frank Jarvis was working at his computer when the email arrived. He was busy putting the finishing touches to the new contracts ready for a meeting the following morning to finalise arrangements for their first collection.

He scratched his head as he read the email and clicked on the attachment. He recognised it all right. Techie wore one like it when he first arrived, to keep his unruly dark curls out of his eyes. How did that get into the pickup?

He carried on with his paperwork, and it wasn't until later, when his son would be taking his lunch break, that Frank phoned him.

"Michael, do any of your friends wear a bandana?"

His son replied in the negative, and asked why.

"It doesn't matter, just wondered," replied Frank, who was relieved but also ashamed at still having that nagging doubt about his son.

He hung up and started to look through his drawers for the business card the detective had left; and finding it, he dialled the number.

THURSDAY 16TH MAY

Afternoon

"Sharon, did you get the address of that web designer?" Cooke asked as he hung up.

"No, I haven't got it yet, as without a good reason the bank won't give it to me. I have looked at his web site and it names him as Jason Black; he is a solo trader and has a BSc (Hons) in Web Design from Huddersfield University. He also has a Facebook page where he advertises his services."

"Get Jimmy to do a search on him. The bandana belonged to him, and although there may be a good explanation why it was in that truck, we need to speak to him pronto. Find out if he has any previous – anything Jimmy can dig up."

"I'll get him on it as soon as he comes in; he's at the dentist having a filling at the moment."

"Tell him to let me know anything he finds straight away. The fact that Black went to Huddersfield University could mean that he has connections in that area."

Something was beginning to take shape in his mind, but he just couldn't grasp what.

He took out the file from his drawer and started to read from the beginning, completely forgetting his lunch order.

He was still reading methodically through all the paperwork when Sharon appeared with a portable Spanish lunch for him: a crusty ciabatta roll filled with Iberian ham, manchego cheese, sliced green olives and sun-dried tomatoes.

He put down the e-mail he was reading and gratefully accepted the delicious offering she had ordered on his behalf.

"Thank you so much, love." He gestured to the paperwork on his desk. "I became so involved in reading this lot, I completely lost track of the time."

She had noticed the mess on his desk and asked if he had found anything.

"No, but something is bugging me. Something I have heard or read is ringing bells but I don't know what. I'm hoping it's in here somewhere."

Finishing his lunch, Cooke threw the paper bag into the bin and set about starting on the untouched pile when his phone rang.

It was Jimmy, who asked if he could come up and speak to him.

Not really wanting to have him in his office, Cooke said he would come downstairs.

"Come on, Sharon, let's go and see what the boy wonder has found."

They both hurried down to the main office, and found Jimmy carefully munching his second breakfast bap of the day. He had made sure to ask the dentist not to use anaesthetic for his filling; he knew where his priorities lay.

"So what have you got, Jimmy-me-lad?"

"Jason Black was in a bit of bother as a teenager, but it seems to have been put down to the fact that his father absconded with a work colleague when he was twelve. A bit of shoplifting, petty theft, that sort of thing. He then seems to have seen the error of his ways, went off to university, and after spending some time working for a local outfit in Huddersfield, set up on his own as a web designer. He turns up again a couple of years ago when he is mentioned in a brawl at a Leeds nightspot. By the time the police arrived it had all settled down and the other man had left. He was rather drunk and a bit abusive but agreed to go home and sleep it off, so it wasn't taken any further."

"Sounds like a one-off blip," noted Cooke.

"I have found out that he runs his business from his home in Halifax," Jimmy continued, handing Cooke the address on a post-it note, complete with greasy thumb print.

"Thanks, Jimmy, good work. I think we need to go and have a word with him, Sharon."

"He could be out at a job at the moment," she pointed out. "The best time to catch him would be this evening."

"Yes, you're right. We'll leave here about three-thirty. That should give us good time to find his place before he arrives home."

Back at his desk, Cooke resumed looking through the paperwork. He had just remembered the email from Dave Akers when Sharon came in waving her car keys.

"Come on, guv, it's time we left."

FRIDAY 17TH MAY

Morning

Last night had been a wasted trip.

Despite a Jag being in the driveway, there had been no one at Jason Black's house, a small one-bedroom terrace in the suburbs. His neighbour, a pretty Asian girl, told them, in a marked Yorkshire accent, that she thought he must be working away as his camper van hadn't been on the drive all week, and she hadn't heard anything of him since the previous Sunday night when he had been out in the garden with some friends. He was usually home at weekends.

This morning Cooke resumed his perusal of the paperwork, which he had left in organised chaos on his desk yesterday.

He started with the email from Dave Akers, which, along with the printout from the local rag, was top of the pile. Reading through he spotted something which he hadn't noticed before and called Sharon over to come and look. It seemed that Carole Black's two brothers hadn't been happy with the outcome of the inquest and had gone on record saying that they blamed her partner. There in black and white were their names, Jason and Andrew.

"It's possible that our Jason Black is her brother. Even more reason for us to go and have a chat with him."

"Certainly sounds likely," Sharon agreed.

"Put his name into HOLMES and see if we can find any connection with Tony Hedges."

"Consider it done," she replied, and set off downstairs to the main office.

It wasn't long before she was back with a printout in her hand.

"There are no links for Jason, but another driver working for the same firm as Hedges is an Andy Black."

Cooke grabbed his notes from the interviews at Grahams transport. Sure enough Andy Black was there. How could he have forgotten him? He was the smelly one.

"I reckon the two of them are in this together," he said. "Yes, look – Andy was off sick on that Monday. Hedges may be involved too and could have picked him up en-route. I'll take Jimmy with me and head off to see Jason this afternoon. Can you ask Gloucester to bring Andy Black in to help us with our enquiries? Take Golding with you to interview him."

Although Cooke would rather have Sharon with him, he wanted to keep the two suspects apart and unable to speak to each other; and he also knew that Sharon wouldn't want to travel all that way with Jimmy in tow.

FRIDAY 17TH MAY

Afternoon

"Grahams Transport, Trevor speaking." The caller identified herself as WPC Shilton. He listened for a moment. "Yes, he is. Should be back about five-thirty after his five o'clock pickup. No, I won't mention it. Okay, see you later."

Craig looked at his manager. "What was all that about?"

"I'll tell you later," Trevor replied and went straight in to see Graham.

When he returned, he looked through the runs that he had prepared for Monday and started to change some of the routes.

Craig knew Tony had a pickup to do in Cheltenham at five this afternoon. Perhaps it was him that Trevor had been talking about.

Another call came in, this time from one of the other drivers who had got to his last drop and realised he had delivered the wrong goods to the previous one.

Craig put him on hold and told Trevor.

"Bloody idiot. That's all I need right now. He'll have to go back and sort it out."

Craig, who had been on early start, passed on the message, and then cleared his desk and left bang on five o clock.

About ten minutes later PC Smith arrived with WPC Shilton, and Trevor showed them into Jenny's office.

Trevor was talking to Leo about his day when Andy walked through the door, so he quickly turned his attention to him, asking him to come through to the office. He walked with him to where the police constables were waiting, shut the door behind him, and went back to finish his conversation with Leo.

"What was that about?" asked his driver.

"I really don't know," answered Trevor in perfect honesty.

Inside the office it was Constable Smith who spoke. "Andrew Black, we would like you to come in for questioning regarding the theft of one of your employer's vehicles on Monday 29th April."

Trevor and Leo watched as they took him away, protesting loudly.

FRIDAY 17TH MAY

Evening

Meanwhile, Cooke and Jimmy Weeks were outside Jason Black's home waiting for his return. The ever-hungry Jimmy had spotted the fish and chip shop in the next street as they passed it and was hopeful of being able to nip back round to get himself some traditional Friday night fare. It wasn't five o'clock yet and Cooke was adamant that they should stay exactly where they were. He didn't want the neighbour to have a chance to speak to Black about their visit yesterday. They didn't have long to wait before they saw the camper van come round the corner at the end of the road. They watched as Black parked it in the drive next to the Jag, which they assumed was his too, and quickly went to apprehend him before he could put his key into the front door lock.

"Jason Black?" asked Cooke.

"Yes. Who's asking?"

"DCI Cooke and DI Weeks, Derbyshire Police." Cooke flashed his ID. "We have reason to believe that you stole a vehicle belonging to Jarvis Chemicals during the weekend of 27th/28th April this year."

Black looked shocked. His eyes shifted frantically from side to side, but seeing there was no hope for escape with Weeks' large form blocking the way, he took a step towards Cooke.

Cooke stood his ground, and realising that his man had intended to flee, he decided to caution him.

"Jason Black, you are under arrest. You do not have to say anything. But it may harm your defence if you do not mention when questioned, something that you later rely on in Court. Anything you do say may be given in evidence."

"Do I need to use these?" Jimmy asked Black, showing him his handcuffs.

"No. I'll come quietly."

Jimmy led him to the back seat of their car and soon they were speeding back to Derbyshire.

On reaching base the two detectives took their suspect to the front desk.

"Escort Mr Black to the interview room please, Sgt Ford."

By now Black was squealing for his solicitor.

Cooke took Weeks to one side and together they decided how they would interview their man once his legal representative arrived.

When Sgt Ford rang through to tell him that the solicitor was now in with Black Cooke sped back downstairs, and collecting Weeks as he went, carried on to the interview room to get the formal discussion underway.

Pushing the button on the tape recorder DCI Cooke stated the date, time, and the names of those present, and then began his questions.

"Can you tell me what you were doing on Monday, 29th April?"

Black took out his diary from the work bag he had brought with him.

"I was working in Milton Keynes for Frank Jarvis."

"On the date in question, he tells me you were not in."

"Of course, I took the day off - had a long weekend - went to London to meet an old girlfriend."

"Can I have her name and address, please?"

"That's a bit difficult. I don't want to get her into trouble. You see she's married."

"I'm afraid you are going to have to if you want to rely on her as an alibi."

"Why do I need an alibi? I've done nothing wrong."

"Is this yours?" Cooke asked, adding for the benefit of the recording, "I'm showing Jason Black the photograph of the bandana."

"I have one like that. Where was it?"

"I'm asking the questions here," Cooke snapped back.

Having stayed quiet so far, Jimmy now spoke up.

"It was in the stolen vehicle and we'd like a sample of your DNA, and your fingerprints, just to eliminate you from our enquiries, of course," he smiled.

Put like this, Black could hardly refuse.

Cooke took over again. "The doctor is here now so we will pause the interview at 19.30 and will resume after she has taken your swab." He turned the tape off.

He and Weeks left the room.

When Sharon and Golding arrived at the police station in Cirencester it was already early evening, and they were shown through to the interview room where Andy Black was drinking a cup of tea. He had already asked for a solicitor, and not having one of his own had agreed to the police solicitor being present to oversee the interview. His fingerprints had been taken, and would be matched against those found on the case of cola at the farm site.

Sharon almost gagged as she entered the room and silently cursed her boss for not warning her. She found herself looking straight at a real-life version of the photo-fit image they had on the white board back at the station. She introduced herself and her companion and turned on the tape. She went through the legal formalities.

"Andrew Black, can you tell me what you were doing on Monday 29th April?"

"Working, I should think."

"Your employer tells us you rang in sick that day.

"Ah yes. It was a twenty-four-hour bug. I was in bed all day."

"Can anyone vouch for this?"

"No. I live alone." Then he added, "I was back at work the next day though."

"How long have you worked for Grahams Transport?"

"Just over a year."

"Where did you work before?"

"I drove for Renshaw's in Halifax." He was clearly wondering where this questioning was leading.

"Do you own a Hazchem licence?"

"Yes."

"Can I see it please?"

Black reached into his trouser pocket, withdrew a wallet and handed over the licence.

Sharon studied it and found that it was in date. She described it for the benefit of the tape.

There was a knock at the door and a constable came in with a piece of paper which he handed to Golding and quietly left.

He looked at it and handed it to Sharon.

She read it, and then set it down. "Can you explain why your fingerprints are on a case of cola which was found in a barn near Leeds where your work colleague, Tony Hedges, was kept prisoner?"

"I must have moved it in our yard."

"There was no delivery of Cola on Hedges' vehicle."

Andy Black was lost for words, so Sharon continued, "This puts you well and truly at the premises where your work colleague was detained, and no doubt your DNA will be on the cigarette butts which you carelessly threw down outside the premises."

Black looked down at his hands

I believe that you abducted Tony Hedges and stole his vehicle, which was carrying a chemical which you had obtained through your brother. You then used that vehicle to dispose of the body of Richard Fox."

"Body? What body? I don't know any Richard Fox."

"Come on, Mr Black, you can do better than that. Mr Fox, as you well know, was the man you blamed for the death of your sister."

"It was all his idea," Andy broke down.

"Whose idea – your brother Jason's?"

"Yes. He said he only needed me to drive the lorry, but..."

"Tell me what happened, Andy."

Back in Derbyshire, Jason's swabs and fingerprints were soon taken and were sent through to be checked against samples found on the van and with hair found on the bandana. Cooke and Jimmy resumed their seats opposite Black and his solicitor.

"Now, where were we?" Cooke asked after switching the tape back on, "Ah yes, the bandana which was found in the van stolen from Jarvis Chemicals."

"I've remembered: I lost my bandana while I was working there. Anyone could have picked it up and put it in the van. I've never been in any of their vehicles so that won't prove anything," Black announced with a smirk.

"Maybe," Cooke agreed. "You said you were in London that weekend at the end of April. I still need the name of the lady you were visiting."

"It was Patricia Coles," he replied and gave them her mobile number. "She should tell you I was there but she may not admit it because of her husband."

Cooke told him they would certainly be checking it out.

"Do you know a man by the name of Richard Fox?"

"Yes, he was my sister's partner."

"Why do you say was? Have they split up?"

"Because he killed her, that's why. Couldn't have a fag outside like she always asked him to. No, he had to sneak his ciggie by the open window." It was clear that Jason Black was becoming agitated and there was pure hatred in his voice as he spoke.

"Is that why you and your brother decided that he had to die too?"

"I don't know what you are talking about. What's this got to do with a stolen vehicle?"

"The chemical stolen with the van was the same as the one used to dispose of Mr Fox's body, and I don't believe in coincidences."

At this the solicitor, Edward Knolls, spoke for the first time.

"It seems to me that you have circumstantial evidence at most, and I suggest that unless you intend to charge him, you allow my client to go."

Cooke knew that the sand was slipping through the hourglass. He was certain that this man in front of him was involved in the death of Richard Fox but knew that without vital, concrete evidence, he couldn't prove it.

"This is a murder enquiry, Mr Knolls, not just the theft of a van."

"Can you leave me to talk to my client, please?"

"I'll give you ten minutes." Cooke turned the tape off again and he and his colleague left the room.

He had got as far as the bottom of the stairs when his mobile rang.

Sharon had lost no time in getting a signed statement from Andy Black and filled Cooke in with the details.

When he and Jimmy returned to the interview room, his first words were, "I have just taken a phone call from my colleague, who is at present in Gloucestershire, where she has been talking to your brother Andrew. He has confessed everything and has named you as the brains behind the whole thing."

"Bloody halfwit!" he cursed, as he stood up and threw his work bag across the room in frustration before collapsing back onto his chair.

Cooke formally charged Jason Black, and he was taken to a cell.

MONDAY 20TH MAY

Morning

Cooke strolled jauntily into the main office.

"Well done, everyone," he said. "We now have two men in custody."

"What was it all about, then?" asked Sgt Ford.

Cooke settled down on the corner of a desk. "Jason and Andy Black had never forgiven Richard Fox for the death of their sister, who they had both idolised. Their conversations often involved how they could get even with him.

"When Jason started setting up the website for Frank Jarvis he became aware that the chemical that they were shipping to hair salon businesses, although perfectly harmless on its own, produced a gas if it leaked which was highly volatile when it came into contact with a flame or another otherwise totally harmless substance. An idea started to form in his head, and when he spoke to his brother next, they came up with a plan.

"Andy had stumbled across Richard Fox's whereabouts some time before, when he had delivered goods to the next industrial unit and saw him leaving Bennetts Clothing. It had been his last drop of the day and he was able to follow him and find out where he lived.

"Andy knew that his work colleague, Tony, always delivered to Yorkshire on a Monday. Jason could steal the chemical and bring it up to Gloucestershire at the weekend; he had borrowed the spare keys from Frank's drawer one day when he was not there and had copies made. As luck had it a pallet had been loaded up on the vehicle he was going to take which made it all the easier for him. Jason set up a fake chemical business from where they could get it picked up by Tony and delivered to them at an abandoned site they knew near Leeds. They would then also have the vehicle to kidnap their quarry. They used Andy's fast BMW to get to Leeds after dumping the van and were ready for Tony when he arrived. Jason sneaked up behind Tony and rendered him unconscious with chloroform, and together they dragged him into the building and locked him in. They left coke and crisps for him, as they didn't mean him any harm and intended to release him. There was no way he could identify them, after all.

"Andy took the lorry to Wellsend, broke into the back of Richard Fox's house and was there waiting for him when he got home from work. He knocked him out in the same manner as Jason had Tony, then fetched a wooden crate from the lorry into which he bundled his tied up and gagged prisoner. Later that evening he wheeled it out through the front door to the vehicle with sheets hiding Richard from view, so when he bumped into the man who had been walking home from the pub, there was nothing on show.

"He drove off to the quarry he'd found last summer while delivering up that way and looking for somewhere to take his lunch break, threw hydraulic oil into the back of the wagon, and punctured one of the bottles of peroxide, which would create a build up of combustible gas and before long a chemical reaction would cause a massive explosion and fire. Jason was waiting with Andy's BMW near the end of the track and Andy took him to

Milton Keynes before heading back to Gloucestershire in time to start work.

"Good job, everyone. I think a drink is in order," Cooke announced. "Meet tonight in the King's Head at seven. The first round is on me."

This was met by cheers from his team.

"But in the meantime, work returns to normal. We need to concentrate on the spate of burglaries in Matlock."

TUESDAY 28TH MAY

Morning

Tony Hedges had set the alarm for an earlier start this morning. He kissed his wife and left for work with a heavy heart.

The weather for the bank holiday had been perfect and he had spent an idyllic day with the family on the Malvern hills.

"Hello, Trevor," he greeted his manager, who was poring over a worksheet on his desk.

"You're early, Tony. I'll be with you in a minute."

Tony waited patiently at the counter while Trevor made some adjustments to the notes on his desk.

"Okay. You'll be wanting your run."

"Yes, but I'd also like a word with Graham if that's all right."

"I'll go and ask."

Trevor gave a courtesy knock before entering the office.

"Tony would like a word, boss."

"Oh?" Graham came out to the counter, and opening the door beside it bade Tony to come through to his office.

"What can I do for you, Tony?" he asked as he offered him a chair.

"This is really difficult and I don't know where to start."

"I always find that the beginning is the best place."

"Well, to be honest, I have never really been happy since

the business in Leeds, especially with it being a colleague – someone I thought was a mate – that used me like that."

Graham nodded and waited for him to continue.

"I have spent a lot of time talking to Sue, and now that she is working, we think we should be able to manage if I took a drop in pay."

"So you want to do less hours? Maybe give up on the nights out?"

"No. I want to go back to farming. I loved working with animals, and at least you know where you are with them."

"Oh. So you are looking for a new job?"

"Not exactly. I have already been offered one, at a large concern up near Stow on the Wold. It's a mixed farm with cows, sheep and pigs, and a few fields of arable. I would love it, and have decided to accept the position. I'd like to leave at the end of next week."

"Well, I can't say I'll be happy to see you leave, lad, but I understand how you feel. It can't have been easy for you or your family. A fresh start, eh?"

"Yes, a fresh start. Speaking of which, I'd better go and get started on today's load."

Graham got up so see him out.

"I wish you all the best."

As he sat down after Tony had left, Graham contemplated how the murder of someone miles away could affect the lives of so many other people – good people – who never even knew him. The world was not what it was when he had started out with a Ford Transit, all those years ago.

Well, they were going to be two drivers down in a week's time, not just one. They had better start advertising.

Printed in Great Britain
by Amazon